VENTAS

55 Great Places
To Eat In The Country

BOB CARRICK

SANTANA BOOKS

VENTAS is published by Ediciones Santana S.L., Apartado 422, 29640 Fuengirola (Málaga), Spain. Tel. 952 485 838. Fax 952 485 367. E-mail santana@vnet.es.

First edition published in 1998.

Photography by Ruth Carrick.

Maps by Jon Harper 1998 ©.

Printed by Gráficas San Pancracio S.L., Poligono Industrial San Luis, Calle Orotava 17, Málaga, Spain.
Depósito Legal: MA-1.167/98   ISBN: 84-89954-03-8

The author would like to thank
the following fearless feeders:
Daphne and Terry
David
Dennis
Dicky and Chris
Heather and Trevor
Jo and Ron
Lynda and Jeff
Olwen
Wilma and Bud
and of course Ruthie
who did all the hard stuff.

CONTENTS

INTRODUCTION

My favourite theory concerning the origin of southern Spain's ubiquitous rural eating places known as ventas is that they arose from that oldest of economic forces, demand and supply. Back in the days when much of the region's seasonal work and big one-off jobs were done by itinerant labour – the theory goes – cheap, hearty meals were in demand. There were few conventional restaurants and they were expensive and not really suitable for working men right off the job. Some enterprising country housewife saw the opportunity, nailed up her shingle offering *Comidas en Venta* (Meals for Sale) and *vaya!* the venta was born.

Or whatever. What matters is that ventas exist, and for that we should all be grateful. For that and for the fact that we are here in Andalusia, as you read this, because the venta is predominantly, if not uniquely, Andalusian. Drive north and you will rarely see the word on an eating place beyond Jaén province.

Most ventas share certain characteristics. They are almost always family owned and operated. They are entirely informal, and tend to be friendly to strangers. The food served is uncomplicated, abundant and, with few exceptions, very good. Don't get the idea, however, that one venta is a carbon copy of all the others because each one has a distinctive personality. Like snow flakes, they are all alike ... but all different.

The venta provides one of the best values for money when it comes to eating out in Spain. A good hearty meal is usually attainable for half the price you would pay in a conventional restaurant. The first course--you are not obliged to order more, if that's all you want--is often a meal in itself for a moderate eater. This course is usually a soup, an egg dish or a light stew. The main course normally offers a choice of steaks, chops, chicken, fish or a casserole. Salads of the lettuce/tomato/onion/olive variety are always available as are fancier models usually adorned with tuna fish and hard-boiled eggs. If you want a dessert, you are probably not in a very good venta (you should be too full), but they usually run to fruit, commercially produced *flan* (Spanish caramel custard) or something similarly uncomplicated.

Sometimes you will see the words *casera* or *hecho en casa* following the name of the dessert--usually custard or rice pudding--which mean that the dessert is home-made. However, that is not a guarantee of superior quality; it just improves your odds. Commercially packaged ice cream confections are often offered in ventas, but they tend to be relatively expensive.

House wines vary, of course, but most are young vintages from Valdepeñas and are usually quite compatible with the rustic menus. A good idea is to try a glass first and if you don't like it, order a bottle of something a bit more upmarket with your meal. Some ventas have surprisingly extensive wine lists, occasionally superior to those found in many seaside restaurants. From our experience, however,15 to 20% of ventas have no wine list at all, though nearly all have some selection of wines of varying quality available at a range of prices.

We usually go to ventas for lunch, anywhere from 1pm to 4pm, never forgetting that business picks up substantially between 2 and 3pm, which is the time most of the

Spanish customers arrive. Some ventas open early in the morning and much of what is on their menus is available whenever the customer wants it. Nearly all of them remain open late and food is usually available right up to closing time.

Unless otherwise noted, the ventas in this book open not later than noon and serve food until 9pm or later. If you are planning to go at an odd hour, it's always a good idea to telephone first to be sure you can be served at that time. Most ventas are closed one day a week (usually mid-week; Mondays for those specializing in seafood), but some are not. Sundays tend to be busy--and noisy--especially on nice days from fall to spring, when the beaches are deserted and local urbanites are looking for a little rural relaxation.

As with most things one does in this country, some knowledge of Spanish is useful when one visits a venta, since most of the waiters do not speak other languages and sometimes menus are recited and not printed (where possible, we tell you what to expect in this regard). It can become confusing trying to remember the names of 20 dishes or more, many of which require definition, and coping with the explanation of the contents of a *puchero* or a dish of *callos* can put a severe strain on a rudimentary Spanish vocabulary. Limited Spanish, however, should not be considered an absolute deterrent.

Presumably you are in Spain for something other than fish and chips or a Big Mac and getting out amongst country people and trying to communicate won't hurt you. There's no record so far of a foreigner starving to death in a venta.

There are a couple of misconceptions concerning ventas. The first is that all venta food is pretty much the same and, therefore, once you have found a venta you like there is no point in going to any others. Wrong. When we were researching this book, we visited more than 70 places we thought might qualify for inclusion and, among the various helpers and my wife and I, we had more than 200 completely different food items. Furthermore, certain things – pork ribs, for example--are prepared so differently from one place to another, that they are, in effect, different dishes, raising our total variety to more than 300 items.

The second fallacy about ventas is that all you have to do when you want your bill is to ask for it. You could even expect the bill to come the moment you have finished your meal, especially on a sunny weekend or fiesta day when the venta is usually crowded. Wrong again. Whatever the reason – my guess is that the country folk who run ventas consider it bad manners to rush the bill to their customers – you will never be brought a bill before you ask for it and, even when you do, they will wait anything up to 30 minutes before bringing it. So what do you do? Well, other than insist you are in a great hurry and need your bill immediately, you can always remember not to empty the wine bottle with your meal so that you have something to sip while you are waiting.

In case you are wondering, there was only one way for a venta to get mentioned in this book, which was – in the combined opinion of myself and my helpers – it served good food and drink, in reasonably comfortable surroundings, with acceptable service, at a fair price. No venta knew in advance we were coming. No venta personnel knew what we were doing until after the bill was paid and we had to ask our essential questions. No venta paid to get into this book -- and could not have done so -- and no free meals were accepted. We played no favorites for any reason whatsoever.

We hope in this book you find everything you will need to know to begin (or expand) your venta experience, including maps, venue descriptions, names and definitions of house specialties, house wines and our opinions of them, and even a phonetic dictionary-cum-glossary.

The asterisks after a venta's name indicate whether it is inexpensive (*), moderate (**) or relatively pricey (***) as compared to all other ventas. Prices will change, of course, but in mid-1998 when this guide was published this is what the three categories meant to us for a three-course meal, including bread and beverage:

(*) Inexpensive ....900 pesetas or less per person

(**) Moderate ....901 to 1200 pesetas

(***) Relatively pricey ...more than 1200 pesetas.

Covering all of Andalusia would have meant, among other things, producing an unwieldy book, so we limited ourselves to ventas within a short drive from the Costa del Sol. As a kind of bonus, we included five outstanding ventas near or en route to major cities outside the province. If you are in an area we haven't covered, however, look (or ask) for the local tourist office (*oficina de turismo*). Many of the staff in these offices speak English and will give you the names of local ventas as well as other information, sometimes even maps.

As total strangers will say to you as they pass your table in many of these eating places, *"Buen provecho"* (Have a nice meal)...and welcome to the wonderful world of ventas.

An invitation

We invite you the reader to recommend your favourite venta for possible inclusion in the next edition of this guide. Your comments and suggestions are helpful and much appreciated and can be sent to Ediciones Santana, Apartado 422, 29640 Fuengirola (Málaga), Spain.

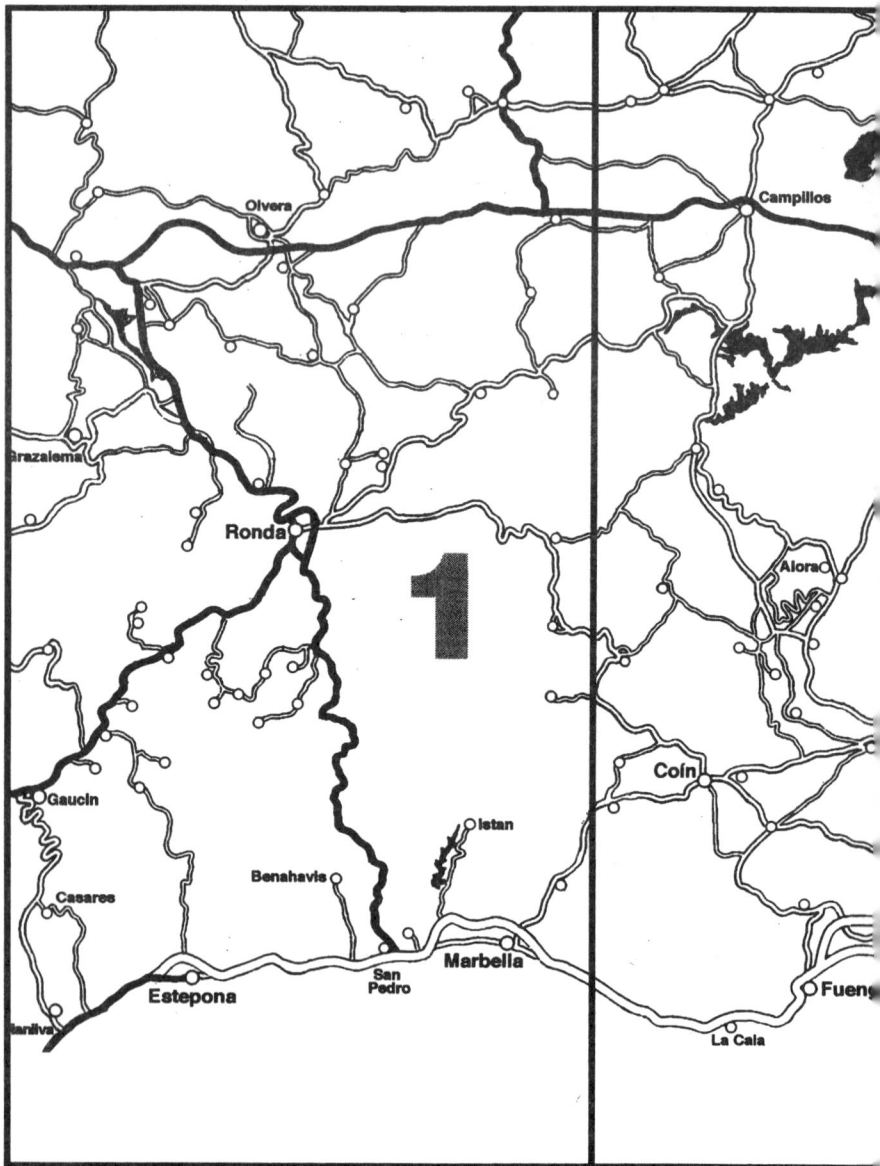

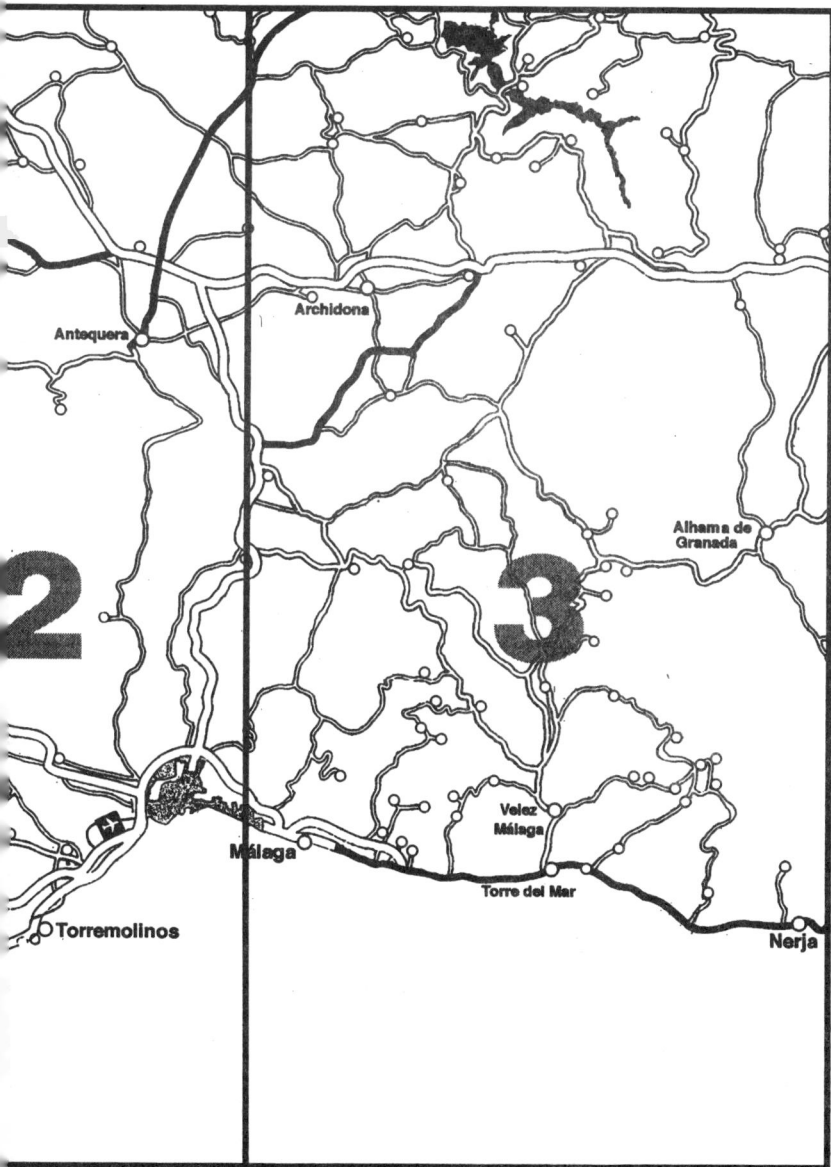

2

3

Antequera

Archidona

Alhama de
Granada

Málaga

Velez
Málaga

Torre del Mar

Torremolinos

Nerja

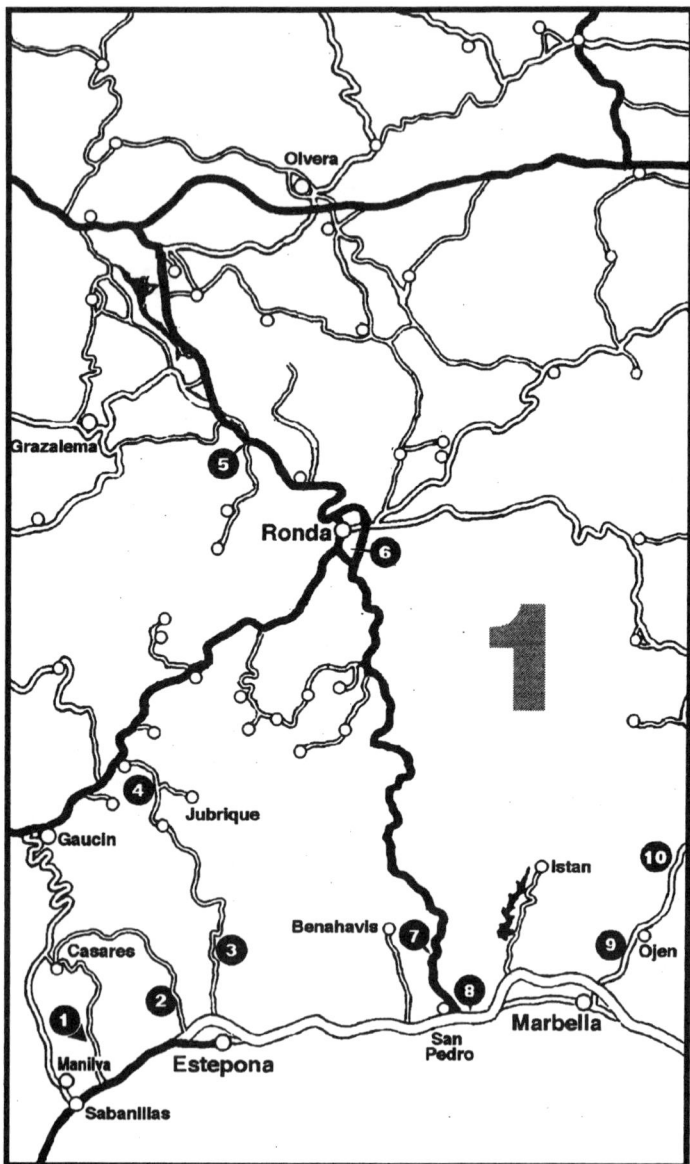

Olvera

Grazalema

5

Ronda **6**

1

4

Jubrique

Gaucin

Istan **10**

Benahavis **7**

Casares **3**

9 Ojen

2

8

1

Manilva

San
Pedro

Marbella

Estepona

Sabanillas

VENTAS MAP 1   **PAGE**

❶ VENTA COZAR **

Carretera Bahia Casares, Km. 4, Casares.
Telephone 952 113 174.
Open year round from 9am to midnight.
Closed Wednesday (after lunch).
Credit cards: Visa, Mastercard, 4-B.

A cook by trade, José Andrés Cozar always wanted his
own business and his dream came true three years ago
when he opened his family-named venta four kilometres
down the unnumbered road which heads north from N-
340 at the development signposted Bahía Casares.

Veteran residents of Estepona recommended the place
and they did us a favour because we had good meals at
very good prices there, with pleasant and efficient service.
And that is what this book is all about.

There's no missing the Venta Cozar. It's all on its own,
right on the road, without another occupied building in
sight, and the name is painted in big, black letters.

You enter from either side directly into the dining room,
a glassed-in square under a cane ceiling. It seats about 70
people. The tables are attractively laid with green and
white undercloths covered with the usual disposable
paper ones.

The principal decor consists of philodendron and other
greenery. With the windows open on all sides, the room
was cool and breezy on the summer day we were there.
Beyond the dining-room is a tiny bar with four tables and
a small fireplace. It looks as though it would be cozy on a
chilly day.

I accepted the recommendation of Señora Cozar, who was waiting tables with the assistance of an agile young-ster, and ordered the lamb chops, a house speciality. There were five of them, good-sized and excellent in all respects, served on a *fuente* (platter), with chips and half a grilled tomato.

It was the meal of the day, however, which impressed us most as outstanding value for money. This began with a first-class *gazpacho*, served with the chopped vegetables already added. The main course was *costillitas de chivo al ajillo* (ribs of kid in a garlic sauce), very tender and tasty meat, served with chips. The dessert was a delicious and generous serving of pears in red wine. This was a fine meal, priced right at the bottom of our intermediate cate-gory, and certainly a bargain.

The house wine was the familiar Peñasol, but we went with a Don Hugo from Alava, which was adequate. The other offerings--very limited--were mostly the popular Faustinos, fairly priced by coast standards but a bit high for an inland venta.

❷ VENTA MANOLO **

Camino de Casares, Km. 4, Estepona.
Telephone 952 794 606.
Open year round from1pm till last customer leaves.
Closed Tuesday.
No credit cards accepted.

The first thing that made an immediate and lasting impression on me on my initial visit to Venta Manolo was one of the coziest and most attractive little bars I have ever seen in a venta. The bar, faced with arab-style tiles, is tiny with just four stools, but even so it has its own small working fireplace, sharing a chimney with the larger one in the dining-room.

Doorways on either side of the fireplace provide entry to the dining-room set up for about 50 diners. It is a plain rectangle with white walls and ceiling, but it instantly grabs one's attention. On the back wall, rendered as if by charcoal on a huge sketch pad, are the larger-than-life figures of a pair of flamenco dancers, the woman in the familiar Seville-style dress and the man in the classic outfit of a Córdoba *caballero*.

On one side is depicted a rural well and on the other a wrought iron gate. Behind the gate is the only touch of colour in the picture – a vase of golden flowers. It is not wonderful art, but it is extremely striking.. Waitress Toni told us that the venta, owned by her father Manuel Martin for more than 17 years, had been until quite recently a *flamenco* venue for years.

Parallel to the dining-room is another dining area, which is a closed-in porch with windows overlooking a green lawn, young palm trees, a country hillside and a small, neat swimming pool.

From an otherwise standard venta menu, I had a house specialty recommended by Toni: a dozen baby pork chops, which were extremely tender. I would have preferred the accompanying chips browner and crisper, but I forgot to ask for them that way.

My companion's meal of the day – *paella*, fried sea bass (served with a mixed salad) and rice pudding- – was a bargain at the very bottom of the moderate price category.

I suggest you give the house wine (Castilla La Mancha) a pass and ask for one of the familiar names on a very short list. They are nothing to fax home about but are more or less fairly priced.

To get there, take the Polígono Industrial exit off the Estepona bypass road. At the top of the exit ramp is a sign pointing to the venta at one and a half kilometres.

❸ VENTA LOS REALES *

Carretera Estepona-Jubrique, C-557, Km 1, Estepona.
Telephone 952 802 646.
Open year round from sunrise to sunset.
No closing day.
Credit cards: Visa, Mastercharge, Eurocard, Access.

Genalguacil is not a major destination for travelers from the coast, which is one reason Los Reales isn't better known, though this classic venta located in the foothills of the Bermeja mountains north of Estepona is popular with local foreign residents and Spaniards for miles around.

If you are coming into Estepona from the east, take the oblique right at the first traffic light, opposite the beginning of the beach. This street will soon intersect with C-557, the road to Genalguacil, where you turn right. Within minutes you will come upon the venta, close to the road on the right-hand side. The modest facade is misleading. The dining room is huge, with room for at least 200 customers.

The Herrera family have owned the venta for 25 years, the ruin next door being the original venta. They have done well with the room decor, considering the large area to be dealt with. The window curtains are a cool, pale green and there are attractive, gilt-framed paintings on the walls.

There are potted green plants in the room's corners and slim vases of fresh flowers on the tables, and diners can enjoy a wonderful view from the long window wall, looking out over Estepona to the sea. There is also room for

about 40 or 50 customers on the covered veranda in front but from here you have no sea view.

The menu, recently printed in English and German as well as Spanish, is large. Rabbit, quail, partridge and even pheasant are listed among the house specialties, but what first brought us here was the roast lamb.

On a recent visit, my companion gave up the lamb and went for the fixed price meal of the day. Her shellfish soup was superior and the sea bass which followed was excellent. With a choice of fresh fruit for dessert, the meal was well within our inexpensive category.

Once again, I was unable to resist the roast lamb and, having been here before, knew I didn't need a starter. The lamb was exquisite as always and so tender that a knife was rarely needed to cut it. My platter was covered with the succulent slices, with a mountain of chips on top.

The house wine is always a Rioja – currently it is Don Darias – and generally it is a cut above what one normally gets in a venta.

❹ VENTA SAN JUAN ✱✱✱

Carretera Algatocín-Jubrique, at Rio Genal bridge, Jubrique.
Telephone 952 152 055.
Open year round from 9.30am till last customer leaves.
Closed Thursday (in winter).
Credit cards: Visa, Mastercard, Tarjeta 6000, Unicaja.

In the dining-room there is a small statue of San Juán put there by the the grandfather of Salvador Aguilar, the current owner of this 70-year-old venta. It's a magical place, 35 kilometers and a million miles from Estepona and the bustling western end of the Costa del Sol.

We drove inland from Estepona on road C-557 and rose through splendid pine and cork forests to Peñas Blancas pass. From the top, on a clear day, five mountain villages are visible.

The venta is located on a hairpin turn right at the Rio Genal bridge. There's not a lot of parking space. We sat in the large dining area, roofed but without walls, separated from the old house containing the kitchen and seldom-used dining room. A few tables were set up in the space between, open to the sky.

The primary house specialties are casseroles of chicken or rabbit with or without garlic. They sounded tempting but we declined because they were advertised as being large enough to serve three people and we were there to try as many dishes as we could at one sitting.

Luckily, the other house specialty category was a big one: anything cooked on the grill. Among the latter offerings I was pleased and surprised to see *picantóns* (young

chickens). I have prepared them many times in my own kitchen but have never before seen them in any kind of Spanish restaurant. Even split and cooked well done on the grill, the San Juan version was delicious.

My companion opted for the *guiso de la casa* (stew of the house), which was listed on the menu as a starter. Her decision not to order anything else for the moment turned out to be a wise one as the delicious "starter" with four generous pieces of pork and a mountain of vegetables would have satisfied at least one hungry stevedore and anything more to eat was out of the question. There was no official meal of the day and putting one together from the menu elevated San Juan to our expensive category.

There was no house wine and none of the wines on the short wine list were cheap enough to be considered as such. The nine reds, three rosés and two whites were all offered at coast prices.

❺ VENTA LA VEGA **

Ctra. Ronda-Jerez (C-339) Cruce de Montejaque, Ronda.
Telephone 952 114 267.
Open year round from 9.30am till last customer leaves.
Closed Thursday.
No credit cards accepted.

We made the trip to Ronda to eat at a famous venta out-side that charming city, but unfortunately it was closed. Luckily we knew of another good establisment in the area called Venta La Vega, a wonderful place run by Mercedes Valle Fuentes for the past 17 years.

Our route to Ronda from the coast was via C-339, which takes off from N-340, just east of San Pedro de Alcántara. This road used to be a nightmare drive with a thousand bends but is now an engineering marvel, providing incred-ible views of mountain valleys and pine-clad slopes. If you are not stopping at Ronda, you bypass the town by con-tinuing on C-339 towards Seville and, some five kilome-tres past the Foreign Legion barracks, you will find Venta La Vega at the Montejaque crossroads.

You enter a little vestibule facing the *servicios*. The bar on your right is the bailiwick of the family son, Amaro, who says he is always there. The air-conditioned dining-room, on your left, is a very pleasant room with about 25 tables fairly close together. The paper table cloths are white on navy blue, with the blue picked up in the bright-ly patterned curtains. The wall decorations are mainly still life reproductions.

When I found out one of the house specialties is *venado en salsa* (venison in sauce), I looked no further, and when the dish arrived I was sure I could not have done better.

It was tender, rich and tasty. And there was a mountain of it. My friend's meal of the day – right at the bottom of the moderate price category – consisted of a good version of Spain's famous *picadillo* soup, an excellent butterflied pork filet and *flan* (caramel custard) made in the kitchen.

The normal house wine was temporarily out of stock, so we had a Castillo de San Ascensio from Rioja for just a bit more and it served well. The are eight reds, five whites and four rosés on the wine list, mostly well-known and mostly at reasonable prices.

Quite apart from its excellent food, pleasant dining room and friendly staff, Venta La Vega is perfectly located for travelers who want to explore this interesting area. It is just a few minutes drive to the pretty town of Grazalema, with its rare Pinsapo pine trees, the Pileta cave, with its famous prehistoric wall paintings, and the Roman ruins at Ronda la Vieja.

❻ VENTA EL MIRADOR *

Carretera Circunvalación (A-376), Km. 123.5, Ronda.
Telephone 952 870 243.
Open year round from 8am to midnight.
No closing day.
No credit cards accepted.

At the very least, eating at the Venta El Mirador in Ronda is a good deal. The food and wine are good, the prices right and the attitude of the Sanchez family, who own and operate the place, is friendly and helpful. To get the best deal out of eating there, however, you've got to have a little luck. For the best deal, you've got to have good weather and one of the few outdoor tables at the back of the building, from where you have a spectacular view of the city two kilometres away.

We got the good weather but, unfortunately, all the outside tables were booked. We had a couple of old friends from southern California with us and we were afraid that eating in the dining-room might seem a bit plebeian to them. With the best will in the world, you would have to say that there is nothing really fancy about the dining-room. It's big and square, seating about 60 customers without crowding.

The decoration consists mainly of high tile wainscoting, posters of Ronda's various attractions and an eclectic selection of reproduced paintings. The 10-stool bar stretching across the entire back of the room was well-patronized but the action there was as decorous as a prayer meeting. There is a huge TV in one corner but, at least during the busy lunchtime we were there, the volume was kept at mini-decibel level.

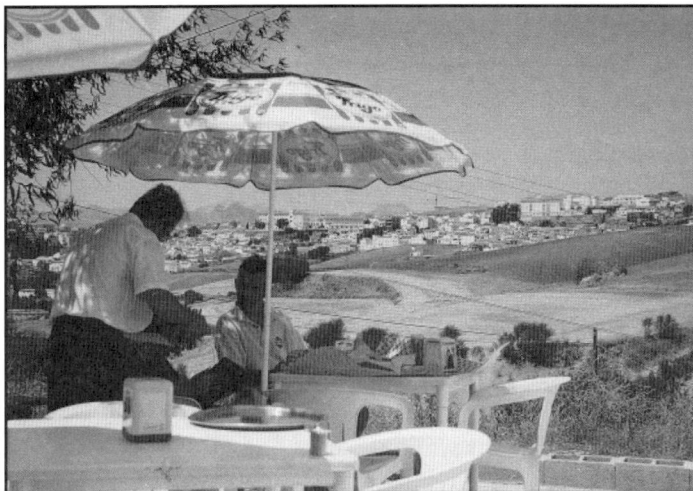

This is a popular place with the locals. A table of Spanish legionaires were having lunch when we arrived and, it being just after two, the dining room was quickly filling up with local folk and Spanish tourists.

One of our party had the inexpensive meal of the day – *callos, albondigas* and a commercial dessert – which we considered very good value. The rest of us had the recommended special of *solomillo relleno* (pork steak stuffed with sausage meat), which was something new for all of us and was delicious and highly recommendable.

We passed on the house wine, which our waiter, family son Valentín, couldn't bring himself to brag about, and tried instead a Campo Burgos crianza 1994 at a very reasonable price. The wine list, it must be said, is small but most tastes and purses can be accommodated.

We needn't have worried about our California friends. Introduced to the Spanish style of sharing a huge salad and exclaiming over the solomillo, they were delighted.

❼ VENTA LOS ALMENDROS **

Ctra. San Pedro–Ronda (C-339), Km. 4, Benahavis.
Telephone 952 786 765.
Open year round from 9am to midnight.
No closing day.
Credit cards: Visa, Mastercard, Eurocard.

It takes very little encouragement for me to try any sort
of wild game dish in a venta, so when I entered the front
door of Venta Los Almendros and found myself staring at
the ferocious countenance of a beady-eyed boar's head
mounted on the far wall, my spirits soared.

Los Almendros has been in business now for more than
a decade, we were told by the son of owner Diego
Fernandez . It was named, he said, for the almond trees
which once grew here in such profusion that the entire
area was known by that name.

Though not far removed from seaside San Pedro's narrow, bustling streets, the dining-room could be that of any
inland Spanish hunting lodge. The boar's head shares
wall space with a dozen reproductions of archaic bullfight
scenes. Two posters advertising notable *corridas* are displayed on other walls.

Over the main entrance are several magnificent drawings of wildlife from Spain's mountains and on the mantle
of the corner fireplace are trophies awarded for proficien-
cy in the use of a shotgun. Fine Iberian hams hang above
the bar situated in another corner.

The printed menu in Spanish and English is large and
surely contains something to suit every taste. Our party of
four had the famous *fritura Malagueña,* a pork tenderloin
steak, chicken in almond sauce and venison. All us were

very pleased with what we got. Fortunately, none of us had starters, else we could not have done justice to the gargantuan main courses. The meal of the day price is well within the moderate range.

The wine list at this excellent venta confused me somewhat. One look at the prices and I ordered the unnamed house red, expecting a modest Valdepeñas. What we got was a litre of Torre del Loro, which was drinkable despite its screw top, but the last thing I expected was a house red from the Costa de la Luz, noted for its fortified aperitif wines and a few table whites. It's no big deal, just strange, but don't let it put you off.

Except for the magnificent view from the terrace, Los Almendros definitely has a masculine flavour. I was a bit worried that the two women in our party might have been uncomfortable with all that overt *machismo*, but they were delighted with the food and the place and were looking forward to a return visit.

31

❽ VENTA EL CASERIO **

Carretera Cádiz-Málaga (N-340), Km. 162, Estepona.
Telephone 952 800 803.
Open year round from 9am till last customer leaves.
No closing day.
Credit cards: Visa, Mastercard, Eurocard.

Located between Málaga and Estepona El Caserío (The Country Home) attracts every sort of patron you can imagine over a lunch period which seems to go on and on. It looks like any country house, except that it is painted an unusual rust colour. There are a few tables on the front veranda. The small, busy bar is on your right as you enter and opposite is a relatively small, pretty dining - room, with blue tablecloths and a fireplace.

No one was in there, so we walked on through to what was obviously the main dining area. This is a big room, under a cane roof, seating at least a hundred people. It was almost full with a colourful mixture of patrons. Beyond a glass wall was another dining area, with a more out-of-doors ambience, covered with a retractable awning.

The menu in Spanish, English, French and German – this is jet set country, remember – contains 47 items, so most tastes should be satisfied. The house specialities are *lomo* (tenderloin, usually pork) and *caldereta de cabrito* (kid stew). I have had the former many times, so I chose the latter, some form of which I have had before, but rarely. It was a brilliant, wise and wonderful choice. My redoubtable companion followed her usual destiny, fearlessly, into the uncharted waters of the meal of the day. This day, that also turned out well. From a large choice, she had *potaje* (soup/stew with meat and most vegetables known to man) and *san jacobo* (breaded veal cutlet).

The house wine is the cheap but perfectly acceptable Don Hugo (with El Caserío's label) from Alava in the Rioja region. The list is surprisingly short for this location but, again, has something for everybody, including a *gran reserva* red at a reasonable price, a couple of decent whites and even a Mateus rosé.

Don't forget that this venta is on one of the main highways in the touristic center of the province. Either avoid going between 1.30 and 3.30pm or be prepared to wait a bit. Make a reservation if you go on Sunday or a holiday.

When Señora Dominga Sanchez, cook and wife of owner Miguel Mena Guerrero, told me the *caldereta* was her grandmother's recipe, not only did I absolutely believe her, I wasn't even surprised. Something that good has to have been around awhile.

❾ VENTA BARRANCO *

Old Coín-Ojén road, Ojén.
Telephone 952 881 191.
Open year round 11am to 10pm winter, midnight summer.
No closing day.
No credit cards accepted.

If you come up from Marbella on the A-355, take the Ojén exit and at the top of the ramp turn left onto the highway overpass. Venta Barranco is on your left a couple of kilometres down the road, and has been there for no less than 30 years.

Barranco offers dining venues for practically every taste. You can sit at one of several tables in the sun, on the open-sided but covered front porch, at one of the six or eight tables in the bar/dining room or, as we did, at one of a few tables in the shade provided by the leaves of a venerable grape vine.

The heat of an August midday was dissipated by a gentle breeze blowing over the adjacent pass. Directly behind us, a separate dining-room used for private functions reminded me of a happy luncheon there a decade before, when I was one of a somewhat tiddly group of British junketeers. This annex, we were told, is still available for such use. It's good to know that not everything changes in the blink of an eye.

Owner Diego Barranco especially recommends the *paella* and the garlic rabbit cooked by his mother, Doña Ana, who is the chef. The rabbit was braised rather than stewed and was delicious and not overpowering, despite the presence of six large garlic cloves in my portion.

The meal of the day, well within our definition of inexpensive, began with *berza* (cabbage, strictly speaking, but around Málaga it is vegetable stew) with the rare main dish offering of *berenjena y huevo* (slices of eggplant dipped in batter and fried, served with a fried egg). Fine summer fare, my companion said.

There's no wine list to speak of, just four reds, including the house Castillo de Montoro, from Murcia, three whites, including the sound Barbadillo, and a couple of rosés. Prices seemed fair.

It seemed likely that the new road from Coín to Marbella would finish off Venta Barranco but when we were there last summer for a weekday lunch, there were six big trucks and two cement mixers parked alongside the road and a parking lot full of cars . It takes more than being cut off by a major highway, apparently, to discourage Doña Ana's fans.

⑩ VENTA PULA *

Carretera Ojén-Monda, Km. 5.5, Monda
Telephone 952 113 068.
Open from 8am to 5pm.
Closed Monday.
Closed for vacation in August
Credit cards: Visa, Mastercard, American Express.

Like many ventas, Pula does not present a pretty face, at least not from the roadside, but it is a very popular eating place – as can be seen from the variety of vehicles and license plates that pack its vast parking area every day (except Monday) after 1pm.

If you go on a Friday, as we did on our last visit, you should go fairly early because Friday is a half-day for most construction workers in the area and from 2pm on things get pretty hectic.

You enter through a narrow bar, which is frequently busy, into a big, square dining-room which seats well over 100 people. The main decoration is the beautiful views from the picture windows on three sides. The front view is of the verdant, tree-covered mountain across the road and the others of the majestic pine trees of the national forest which surrounds the venta. Wisecracking waiter Francisco Vera, a member of the family which has run the business for 12 years, told us the venta had been there for some 20 years.

There were four of us, so we were able to get a good sampling of the menu. The one specialty mentioned by Francisco was a starter, the *sopa mondeña*, full of all sorts of vegetables and bread and very good, as was the *coles con garbanzos* (cabbage soup/stew with meat and chick

peas). Pork loin with eggs, veal stew and grilled hake were all happily devoured by those who went for the meal of the day, which falls into our inexpensive category. The fourth meal was *chuletitas de cordero* (literally, little lamb chops and little they were) with potatoes and mixed vegetables. The five small chops were delicious, however, and quite enough for lunch.

The wine list is small: 10 Rioja reds with familiar names, two whites and two rosés, all at a bit below coast prices. We were happy with the house red, the Vilamar from Jumilla. The price was incredibly low, even by venta standards.

Until recently, Venta Pula was not a place one just happened upon. It was out in the boondocks between Marbella and Coín on a bad road which few people had occasion to travel but, once it established its excellence, more and more people decided it was worth the trouble to get there. Now, with the new network of improved roads, getting to Pula from anywhere on the Coast is easy and pleasant.

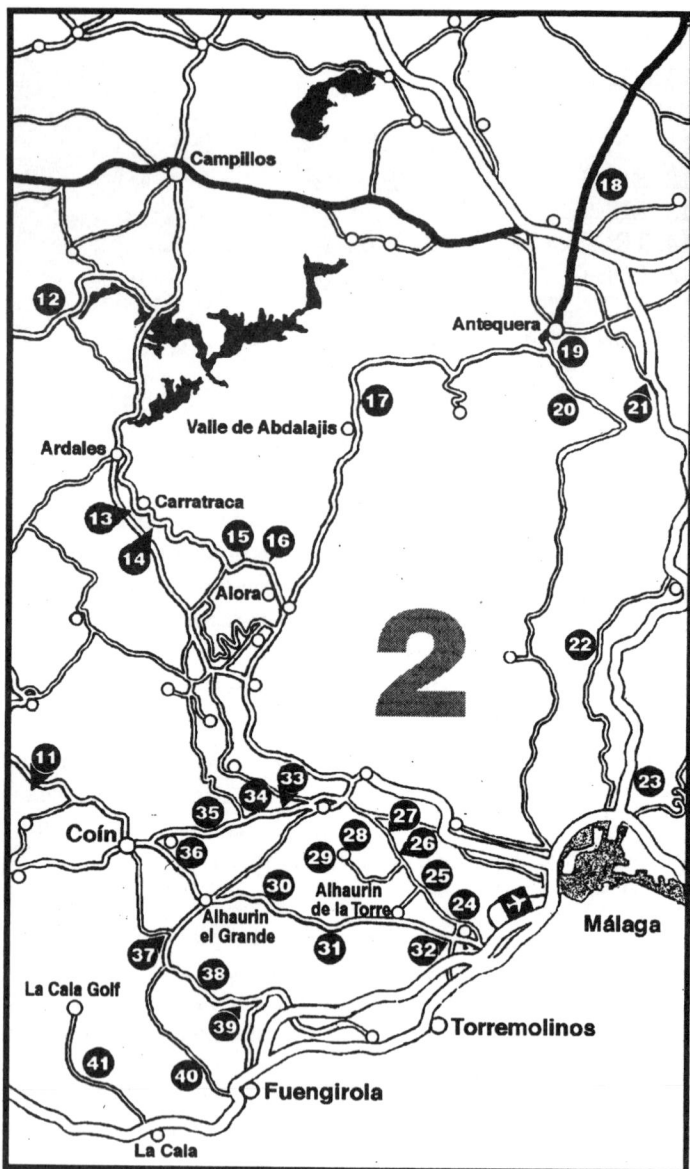

Campillos

18

12

Antequera

19

20

21

Valle de Abdalajis

17

Ardales

13

Carratraca

14

15 16

Alora

2

22

11

33

34

23

Coín

35

36

27

28

26

29

25

Alhaurín
de la Torre

30

24

Alhaurín
el Grande

31

32

Málaga

37

38

La Cala Golf

39

41

40

Torremolinos

Fuengirola

La Cala

⑪ VENTA RIO GRANDE *

Carretera Coín-Ronda (A-366), Km. 52, Coín.
Telephone 952 452 245.
Open year round from 9am to 9pm.
Closed Monday.
No credit cards accepted.

The best-known Rio Grande of course is the one that forms part of the border between Mexico and the United States - the river John Wayne was always riding across - but we have our own Rio Grande right here in Andalusia and it meanders across much of the middle of Málaga province.

I shall never forget the first time I walked across the little bridge that crosses the Rio Grande just below the town of Alozaina. I looked down into the river and saw a huge trout.

The Venta Rio Grande is about five kilometers from that bridge, on the Coín side. It is a great block of a building, obviously designed to attract Spaniards on weekends, holidays and special occasions, which is not to say that anybody else who turns up at any time is not more than welcome.

What can you say about a dining-room that is around 3000 feet square - with a big veranda out front and an even bigger patio out back - except that it's awfully big? There's attractive tile wainscoting on all the walls, greenery here and there, not-so-good reproductions of good Spanish paintings, an extremely large working fireplace set in one wall, several ceiling fans, a cool green-and-white

colour scheme and a 15-stool, L-shaped bar in one corner, thoughtfully screened off from the dining area by latticed room dividers.

After my experience at the bridge, I was hoping to see trout on the menu, but was disappointed. I should not really have been surprised because, come to think of it, you rarely see trout on offer at an Andalusian venta.

On our last visit, the menu (printed in Spanish and English) listed many standard venta items but contained unusual offerings, too. We tried the *muslos de pollo plancha* (grilled chicken thighs) and the *salpicón de bocas de mar* (seafood salad). Our friends had *rosada plancha* (fried sea bass) and *carne mechada* (see glossary). We were all happy with what we had chosen. The meal of the day was advertised at a price which fits our least expensive category.

The house wine was the venerable Soldepeñas. The wine list offered the red Campo Viejo, Romeral and Cumbrero, the white Barbadillo and not much else.

41

⑫ VENTA EL CORDOBES **

Carretera Campillos-Ronda (Km. 19), Teba.
Telephone 952 748 492.
Open year round from 8am till last customer leaves.
Closed Monday (after lunch).
No credit cards accepted.

We heard there were several ventas around the old fortress town of Teba north of Málaga, so we got on the newish A-357 and went up to check them out. We regard this as our own Yellow Brick Road, so magically has it paved the way to an area that was, until recently, something of a mystery.

The new highway ended temporarily some 10 kilometres before the ruined tower of Teba's ancient castle riveted our attention to the horizon, and we found ourselves back on country roads. It was just as well. Needless to say, one slows down and has a better chance to appreciate the simple beauty of Ardales, snuggled up against the hillside on the left.

Venta El Cordobés (named after the bullfighter) was the first one we came to, at the T-junction of our road with the Campillos-Ronda road. After inspecting the others, we came back to it as the probable best bet. A wise choice, we later agreed. It's not terribly prepossessing, but we reckoned that any place which advertises only its air conditioning and its *callos* on the facade, in August, has got its priorities right.

If it's relative peace and quiet you want, you can seat yourselves at one of the half dozen tables on the glassed-in

front porch. Otherwise, enter the bar, where the display of miniature booze bottles begins. Waiter/factotum Manuel, the son-in-law of owner Juan Manuel Perez , has some 800 of them in his collection.

In the small but cosy dining-room (10 tables) you will find a printed menu, in Spanish only, very pleasant people, good service and prices that will make you happy.

The meal of the day, priced at the bottom of our moderate category, offered a huge selection. My companion went for the *callos* and the *calamares fritos*, both of them texcellent. From the house specialities I selected the *conejo al ajillo* and was going to let it go at that, as I often have just one course for lunch. Fortunately, I noticed the *salmorejo* among the starters and ordered that as well. The rabbit was excellent, simmered in oil rather than stewed, as it usually comes. And the *salmorejo*, that burly king of cold soups, was a work of art.

Manuel was frankly unhappy with the house wine and didn't recommend it. From a long wine list – remarkable for a venta, both as to selection and prices – we had a Sonsierra Rioja (1994 vintage) at a very fair price.

⑬ VENTA EL PUNTO *

Carretera Carratraca-Alora (opp. town entrance), Carratraca.
Telephone 952 458 197.
Open year round from 7am till last customer leaves.
No closing day.
No credit cards accepted.

When you have eaten in as many ventas as I have, the one thing you would wager you are not going to find is a completely different salad. Venta El Punto surprised me. The menu said *ensalada de tomates picadas* and to me that meant "minced tomatoes." I had trouble visualizing it. The mental picture came out wet and mushy. "No, no," waiter Miguel Guerrero told me, "it is *tomate con ajo*." And so it was: a large platter of firm, ripe, locally grown tomatoes, sliced into thin wedges and liberally sprinkled with large chunks of raw garlic. Delicious – though your companion had better share it if she is going to ride back in the same car.

Miguel is married to Salvadora Díaz, whose father, now retired, opened El Punto some 15 years ago. They welcome strangers and write out the short list of items to choose from for a meal of the day which fits well within our inexpensive category.

My companion began with the familiar venta item *sopa de puchero*, which we sometimes refer to as "bread soup," though it can be excellent. This one was OK. Then she had the same cubes of meat you get on a stick of pinchitos, except it wasn't on a stick and there was more of it. And then a commercial dessert. She was happy.

In addition to my simple but dazzling "minced tomatoes," I tried the recommended pork ribs. Ribs are done at

least six ways in Andalusia that I know of and this was the one where they are put on a grill over some kind of fire and cooked very brown with little or no basting sauce. Done this way, they are very tasty but usually require some chewing. There were 10 small ones, with lots of chips, and I chewed away quite contentedly.

The wine list is practically non-existent: one or two Rioja reds and a couple of whites with what sounded like Montilla-Moriles names. I went with the house red, the cheap Tomás García which, obviously out of a larger container, came in an unlabeled bottle with a cork stuck in. Surprisingly, it turned out to be quite satisfactory, .

Things proceed at a leisurely pace in Carratraca. Even when the *balneario* (mineral bath) is open during the summer, there doesn't seem to be a mad rush to get to lunch. We did find one advantage to getting to El Punto a bit earlier than others, however. On the veranda, which faces the town, there is just one table to the right of the door. From that table the diner has a unique view not only of the town's immaculate white-washed houses but also of the pine-clad mountain behind it.

⑭ VENTA EL TRILLO *

Carretera Alora-Ardales (Km. 16), Carratraca.
Telephone 952 458 199.
Open year round from 8am till last customer leaves.
No closing day.
Credit cards: Visa, Mastercard, Eurocard, Unicaja.

Manolo Sanchez, cook at Venta El Trillo and son of owner Lucía Gutierrez, believes in keeping things simple. There is a nicely printed menu but during the week there aren't many customers, so only a few of the items are kept on hand. Instead of presenting his working day customers with the menu and having to say "no" to most requests, he writes out what is available that day. When we were there, he was offering four starters, four main dishes and a selection of desserts.

Very practical, we thought. As happens only rarely in ventas, in our experience, he also writes out what's available for the fixed price meal of the day (very cheap): three starters and two *platos fuertes*. In addition to the meal of the day, the other items available were two major steaks–one each of beef and pork – and a leg of lamb.

Having discovered on previous occasions the simple pleasures of Carratraca – easy and pleasant to get to from anywhere on the Costa del Sol – we took some friends from England with us.

We all came to the conclusion, independently, that the heavier meals would be too much on that warm day, so we all opted for the meal of the day. No one felt like fish, so we all had the pork chops, but amongst us we tried both

soups – the *ajo*, it was generally agreed, had a slight edge on the *picadillo* – and the salad, which was a large, superior concoction, crisp, well-dressed and "with no brown bits," to quote one of our British friends. The pork chops, served with lemon quarters, were tender and cooked precisely right. Considering that I had forgotten to give my little "well-browned" speech, the chips which accompanied them were not bad.

Before I could ask for the wine list, a jug of the house red appeared on the table, together with a complimentary dish of olives which had never seen the inside of a canning factory. What with one thing and another, I forgot to ask about the wine's pedigree or even its name. I can say for sure that a couple of jugs of it went down very nicely.

At the end of the meal, Manolo unhesitatingly recommended the only homemade dessert, the *pudin de la casa*, which turned out to be *flan*, but with a very distinctive embellishment. It was topped with mixed fruit and angelica . Whatever, it was a cut way above the usual *flan* and a fine finish to a very enjoyable meal.

A nice touch that made the meal even more enjoyable was Manolo not charging for the second jug of wine. Now there's something I'll drink to.

47

⑮ VENTA LOS CONEJITOS *

Carretera Alora-Carratraca (Km. 5), Alora.
Telephones 952 496 942 and 952 598 007.
Open year round from 9am to midnight.
No closing day.
Credit cards: Visa, Mastercard, Unicaja, Tarjeta 6000, Telebanco.

Looking over the front of the venta, I reckoned Los
Conejitos (The Little Rabbits) could seat 70 or 80 people in
the big, glassed-in veranda in front of the bar and maybe
another 40 or 50 in the two small dining-rooms to one side.
We were there on a beautiful Saturday well into the hunting season and between hunters and local families – no
foreigners that day – it looked like they would lay out at
least 100 lunches. Not bad, I thought, for a little place five
kilometres outside Alora, on a rough road. I hoped they
were making it, because this is the kind of venta I want to
stay in business.

They had just served me two of my favourite dishes –
shrimps in spicy oil, bubbling as it should be, and possibly
the best I have ever had of that most common of venta
dishes, rabbit stewed in garlic. My companion had a local
specialty, *sopa perota*, a vegetable soup/stew with a bread
base, in a big bowl, which was a meal by itself. The prices
were absurdly low. The meal of the day is one of the
cheapest we found.

Taking into account the spectrum of flavours in the food
we had ordered, I picked a *rosado* wine to drink, the Vina
Albali, for me one of the best Valdepeñas vintners. It was
perfect. And it was served in an ice bucket, an almost
unheard-of embellishment in a venta.

The wine list is exceptional as regards both selection and prices. There are more than 20 reds – mostly Riojas, but with a few others such as the famous Torres from Penedés – and six each of whites and rosés, most of them at much lower prices than in many coastal restuarants. This is the best wine list we found in our venta survey.

The chances are that you would never find Los Conejitos without directions. You come right up the main road from Málaga, pass the Alora tourist office and go straight ahead at the stoplight on the old Carratraca road. Five kilometres on you see Los Conejitos on your right.

After lunch, Cristobal Martín, the family member who runs the day-to-day operation, showed me the annex they had built in 1997. That very night, it was to be the site of a wedding dinner for 800 people. In case you think that might be a misprint, that number was eight hundred.

⑯ FUENTE DE LA HIGUERA*

Carretera Alora-Carratraca (Km.1), Alora.
Telephone 952 496 214.
Open year round from 10am till last customer leaves.
Closing Monday.
No credit cards accepted.

It's only a 40-kilometer drive from Málaga city to Alora and, on a nice day, the trip is a scenic one up the valley of the Guadalhorce or, as the Aloreños call it, "the valley of the sun." Indeed, the area has charms and interests enough to have attracted a significant number of foreigners to take up permanent residence. Of several ventas on the outskirts of town, we chose the Fuente de la Higuera (Fountain of the Fig Tree) primarily because of the magnificent view of the valley it gave us to go with our meal.

You park immediately in front of the venta and enter the bar through a tin-roofed veranda with 10 tables. To your right an old grape vine covers a patio which can easily accommodate another dozen tables or more when the weather is benign and which enjoys the valley view.

The bar-room has four six-seat tables where the local workmen tend to eat their lunch. It's a comfortable room with television and vending machines. Beyond the bar is the small formal dining-room, with only one significant decoration – the view, and not everyone gets that.

The menu is large, but that can be misleading. Specialties such as *migas* and the *sopa perotas* are only available when large crowds are expected, as on Sundays or holidays. However, there are plenty of standard items, two of which – the *rosado* (sea bass) and *churrasco* (barbecued meat, usually pork) – we chose and found perfectly acceptable. There are also a few uncommon offerings, such as

the *tomates con anchoas* (sliced tomatoes served with canned anchovies and the house olives) which was delicious and absurdly cheap. The meal of the day is also among the least expensive we found.

The wine situation here is pretty basic. The taste of many of the regular patrons runs to fino sherries and the similar products of Montilla-Moriles. Otherwise, you can get a house wine called Carbonell. I decided to pass on that when I found I could get a Faustino VII or a Campo Viejo at a very reasonable price.

Alfonso Trujillo, who waited on us, is one of the members of the group which rents the building. Their lease runs until the year 2000 and they have no plans to leave. He believes the place has been there for about 30 years.

If you plan to have lunch at the Fuente La Higuera, take my advice and get there not long after 1pm, especially if it is a fine autumn day. Just three tables in the small dining room overlook the lemon orchard to the valley and the distant mountains ... and the meal costs the same with or without the view.

⑰ VENTA LOS ATANORES *

Carretera Alora-Antequera (A-343), Km. 17, Valle de Abdalajís.
Telephone 952 488 068.
Open year round from 8.30am to 9pm.
No closing day.
No credit cards accepted.

The easy drive from the coast up to Alora is scenic enough but the views at Valle de Abdalajís just beyond Alora take your breath away. And that's from the ground. They must be even more stunning for those daring young fliers gliding like eagles above the mountains and lakes. They dot the sky – for this is paragliding country.

We found out about this at the Venta Los Atanores (arab for water pipes) where people from the paragliding school hang out. You can get all the details about this exciting sport right there. You can also get a good meal in pleasant surroundings.

We were there on an early winter day and there was a distinct chill in the air, which made the wood fire in the dining-room fireplace very welcome. It's a ten-table room separated from the bar by the usual lattice-work divider. The main decorations are painting reproductions and ceramic plates.

There is a meal of the day and it is inexpensive, but our waiter Francisco José Rosa Gomez, son of the owner, made it clear that the management considers that to be a special deal for the workers. We didn't push it and had, instead, the two house specialities, pork loin and rabbit in garlic. To quote my lunch mate, the pork was "tender, tasty and served with a perfectly fried egg." My rabbit

contained a lot of liver and was very rich. It was served with much of the olive oil in which it was cooked, which I am sure is not to everyone's taste, but is very much to mine. We also had two wonderful starters, *cazuela de patatas* (potato stew, with meat) and *migas* (fried, spiced bread and bacon bits), an Andalusian specialty which can be much better than it sounds, which this serving was.

As is often the case in ventas, there was no wine list, but when I asked for the house red I got a very palatable though very young Abadía de Altillo from Rioja for a price we have often paid for a house Valdepeñas.

Congenial owner Francisco Rosa Castillo confided that the paragliding activities have meant an increase in his business, especially among non-Spaniards, and was influential in his decision to construct a hostal on top of the restaurant. He has already added a 500-seat dining-room in back to accommodate weekend trade, which was scheduled to open the weekend following our visit.

⑱ VENTA LOS PILOTOS **

Carretera Antequera-Córdoba (N-331), Km.116, Antequera.
Telephone 952 844 934.
Open year round from 8am to midnight.
Closed Tuesday.
Credit cards: all major credit cards accepted.

Asked why he had named his place Los Pilotos, Juan Velazquez, a big, bluff man who enjoys a joke with the truck drivers who frequent his venta, told me: "Well, we're all pilots, aren't we? You're an automobile pilot, these boys are truck pilots...and then there are the students at the flying school out back who are learning to fly ultra-lights."

The only way you can get into Venta Los Pilotos is through a medium-sized bar with a counter running its entire length, over which hang at least 100 serrano hams. You can buy one if you want. Crowding the bar space somewhat is what could well be the world's largest gum-ball machine and one of those games where you try to pick up a prize with a minature crane. The truck pilots seem to like the atmosphere.

The ambience inside the hunting-lodge-style, beam-ceilinged dining-room is completely different – sedate and quiet. During our late "lunch" there was a group of elderly, well-dressed Spaniards, two separate commercial travelers and us. The truckers hung happily in the bar.

There is no wine list and I was invited to inspect the large racks on the back wall – all reds – and take my pick.

The only white table wine on offer – perfectly chilled, I must say – was Antonio Barbadillo's Castillo de San Diego, from Cadiz. That suited me, even though I paid a Coast price for it.

The wine went well with the house specialty, grilled Iberian pork chop. The two generous chops were smoky-flavoured and excellent, served with a potpourri of steamed vegetables. The meal of the day chosen by my companion was shellfish soup, what appeared to be baked ham chunks lightly flavoured with garlic, followed by a custard made in the kitchen. It was almost as good as my chops and was a great bargain in the moderate price range. The menu in Spanish only is large and fairly priced.

⑲ VENTA EL MIRADOR*

Carretera Antequera-Torcal, Km. 0.5, Antequera.
Telephone 952 844 523.
Open year round from 9am to 8pm winter (later in summer).
Closed Monday.
Credit cards: Visa, Tarjeta 6000.

If ever a place was appropriately named it is El Mirador
(The Viewpoint), which offers an incomparable panorama
of Antequera from the south and Lovers' Leap, a tall bluff
from which a star-crossed Moorish girl and her Christain
lover, forbidden by their parents to marry, chose to jump
to their deaths rather than be parted.

It really is too bad that weekday customers can only
enjoy that splendid view from the venta's parking lot.
There is a dining-room and an adjacent balcony which display it wonderfully but, for some inexplicable management policy , they are sealed off except for weekends, holidays and special occasions. Never mind. The food is
good, the prices are reasonable--the meal of the day is well
inside the inexpensive category--and you can pause on
your way in or out to admire the scenery.

The menu is enormous, with more than 50 items listed,
not counting desserts, so we were glad there were four of
us on our last visit, so we could make a fair sampling of
what owner Antonio Munoz had to offer from his kitchen.
My three companions each had a different meal of the day:
callos and *sopa picadillo* (both of which should sound
familiar by now) and s*opa de alubias* (navy or haricot

bean soup), followed by pork chop, pork fillet cooked with garlic and a stuffed pepper.

I was delighted to learn the pig's knuckle is a house speciality and if I had known what an enormous joint I would be given, I would have been able to resist the *porra antequerrana*, one of my favourite starters. The meat-- there was almost no fat--fell off the knuckle and it was served with a tart brown sauce which made the whole dish a memorable experience. All of us came away from the table well-fed and happy.

There was no wine list, though Faustino, Paternina and Marques de Riscal were available. We had the house wine and wound up with the familiar Soldepeñas red and a Don Rodrigo white from Badajoz, which wasn't at all bad.

Antequera is a beautiful town, easily accessible from anywhere on the coast and inexplicably overlooked by many tourists. It has numerous natural, architectural and artistic attractions which warrant at least a one-day visit. If you go, there is no better place than El Mirador to eat lunch, relax and take a look at the big picture.

㉔ VENTA LA RIVERA

Carretera Antequera-Torcal, Km. 3, Antequera.
Telephone 952 703 003.
Open year round from 10am till last customer leaves.
No closing day.
No credit cards accepted

We thought we knew the venta scene around Antequera. We went up to add one to the list--there are several good ones there--and suddenly we saw this enormous venta where we would have sworn there wasn't one two weeks before. We were right. La Rivera had opened its doors just 13 days before. Unlucky for some, perhaps, but not for us. We ate like hungry lumberjacks for a price which, at best, would buy soup, sandwiches and an occasional bad attitude on much of the seaside Costa del Sol.

You can't miss La Rivera. The big, black letters spelling out its name are big enough to stop your vehicle in its tracks. Inside, it's a big barn of a room set up for about a hundred customers but with room enough for many more if needed. The bar, stretching across the kitchen end of the room, is separated from the dining area by a lattice screen. The action would have to get pretty rowdy before it would bother the diners.

Considering it is so new, lessee Juan Pedro Fuentes and his family have made good progress in giving the place some personality. The bright red table cloths and the Alpujarra curtains help. A large mirror adorns one wall and there are ceramic plates here and there. There is also a large still life painting with an El Torcal background, a fireplace, and air conditioning.

La Rivera has a large menu (in Spanish only) and the food is not only good, the portions are very generous. My lunch companion had the meal of the day – inexpensive by our criteria – consisting of *migas* (a big enough serving to require my help) and the *plato combinado* (a pork chop, egg and potatoes). Good truck driver's grub. For considerably less cost, I had one course only, the *parillada de carne* (mixed grill), with enough meat and potatoes to banish all thoughts of a dessert.

There is no wine list and only an eclectic half dozen bottles to choose from. Faustino VII was the only one I had heard of. I got lucky in trying an Alavesa Rioja named Covila which despite being just a year old was not bad and extremely cheap.

I suggest that you get up to La Rivera while you can still get something like a pound of meat for the price of less than the meal of the day in any venta in which we have eaten. It can't last.

㉑ VENTA LA YEDRA**

Autovía Málaga-Córdoba (N-331), Km. 136, Antequera.
Telephone 952 701 497; Fax 952 842 287.
Open year round: restaurant 1-4, 9-11pm (bar stays open).
No closing day.
Credit cards: Visa, Mastercard, Eurocard, American Express.

If you drive toward Córdoba, you will surely see La Yedra (The Ivy) with its imposing facade and boldly-painted name. When I first entered the big main door I did so with some trepidation because it looks so much like those bar/cafeteria/hostal combinations one sees in central and northern Spain. They are usually located either at a major crossroads or so far out in the boonies it's a long distance call to the next eating place. They are soulless places with coffee cups lined up along a 30-metre bar, ready for the stream of truck drivers or bleary-eyed civilians in need of a caffeine fix.

I need not have worried. What we found instead – at least in the main dining-room - was a big warm and friendly room with dark woodwork, seating upwards of a hundred people at comfortably spaced tables and a surfeit of uniformed waiters. You rarely get uniformed waiters in a venta and I wondered if this elegance would be reflected in the prices but they were no more than most of the ventas we've been to and less than some. Meal of the day was priced at the top of our moderate category.

We chose from a comprehensive menu (in Spanish only). My lunch companion had two of the house specialties, *cocido andaluz* (Andalucian vegetable soup/stew),

which she said was delicious, and an enormous piece of pork tenderloin, which we agreed (I got to taste) was as tender as any meat we have ever eaten...and beautifully flavoured. I had the trout prepared Navarra style (that is, served with serrano ham). It was a big brute presented and cooked better than in some places which specialize in that particular fish.

We decided on a white wine with fish and pork. A Faustino VII from a comprehensive list – at more or less coast prices – served well.

After lunch last December, we lingered over coffee. There was the head of a fine buck over the working fire-place, the antlers of several others on the wall, two enormous Elizabethan bronzes beside the chimney and – I swear – snow in the fields visible through the huge front windows. It felt more like a Bavarian hunting lodge than a venta 35 kilometres north of Málaga capital.

㉒ VENTORILLO PATASCORTAS ✱✱✱

Camino Real, 8, Casabermeja.
Telephone 989 663 168.
Open year round from 12 noon to 11pm.
Closed Monday.
No credit cards accepted

Ventorillo means the same as venta. *Patascortas* (Short feet) is an ancestral nickname in the family of owner Miguel Campoy. The building and the location have a long history-cum-legend which has been researched by Miguel and his wife Loli, who have been operating the venta only since 1996. On display is a three-page story in Spanish which traces the building back to the 15th century and the courtyard to Roman times.

Bright red and yellow signs point the way, the first of which appears as you enter Casabermeja from N-331, the main highway north from Málaga. From the rather small parking area, you enter a courtyard with some half dozen tree-shaded tables overlooking a valley and, on a clear day, Málaga and the Mediterrean. You can spend some pleasant moments here admiring the view, possibly in the company of a burro named Pavarotti, or have a drink at the tiny bar just inside the door. Thirty to 40 patrons can be accommodated in the strikingly decorated dining- room.

The very short menu does not include a meal of the day and the cheapest one you can put together--picadillo soup, pork chops, fruit in season and half a bottle of the house wine--makes it expensive by our definition, but not by a lot. Whatever you eat – and the food is certainly

good and plentiful – it's well worth the price for the pleasure of enjoying the surroundings and tasteful decorative touches of Miguel and Loli.

A friend knew the venta and ordered our meal in advance. It began with salad and large platters of fried anchovies and two kinds of fried sausage slices. Because he had ordered the fish, our host requested that the *paella* contain only pork, which it did in quantity. It was delicious, though I would have preferred it Málaga style, which includes shellfish.

The wine list was still in preparation, but a small selection, mostly Riojas, was available at coast prices. Ours, an Olarra Añares 1994, went very well with the spicy food.

Patascortas is an experience too good – and too close at hand – to miss. Take a pleasant drive through scenic countryside, have a drink while admiring the views, and enjoy a good meal in tasteful surroundings. And don't forget to take your camera.

㉓ VENTA COTRINA *

Carretera Malaga-Antequera (N-331), Km. 160, Málaga.
Telephone 952 652 350.
Open year round from 7am till midnight.
No closing day.
No credit cards accepted.

The N-331, the main road from Malaga to Antequera and points north, must surely be the most heavily traveled road in and out of the provincial capital. There are at least half a dozen ventas on this road before it reaches Casabermeja and I felt we had to include at least one example of these equivalents of what in America are called "truck stop cafes."

We picked Venta Cotrina, the first eating place to be opened (in 1970) on this highway after it was completed. The word Cotrina has no meaning in Spanish, but Cristobal, who waited on us and who has some tenuous family connection with Maria Moreno, the owner, says that there was a famous local farm called Cotrina as far back as 300 years ago and that the whole area is still known by that name.

No matter whether you are heading north or south, Cotrina is easily accesible through a highway underpass. The place is right on the highway, but set back just far enough so that traffic noise isn't much of a problem. Don't worry about the limited parking spaces visible. There's a large parking area in back.

There are several choices of eating areas in Cotrina – an open partly shaded terrace, a big glass-enclosed room beside it, and the bar. Both the latter are air-conditioned.

Asked about the house specialities, Cristobal said the
lomo en manteca would come immediately and the *paella*
would take 20 minutes. Not wanting to wait, we both had
the lomo, a large chunk of extremely tender pork cooked,
as is the usual custom with venta *lomo*, in orange grease
and served with a mountain of chips. For starters my
companion had a *potaje* which, loaded with pieces of chick-
en and pork and a garden's yield of vegetables, was almost
a meal in itself. There was no meal of the day and the one
we put together ourselves worked out at the top of the
least expensive category.

Cotrina isn't the sort of place that has a wine list. If you
don't fancy the house wine, the popular Peñasol, you have
a very few Riojas to choose, but beer by the litre is cheap.

A busy highway certainly isn't the ideal setting for a
meal out, but if it's a good, cheap meal you want you could
do worse than do what the Malagueños do (not to mention
lots of truck drivers) and stop at Venta Cotrina.

㉔ VENTA EL.POZO *

Carretera Churriana-Cártama, Km. 0.7, Churriana.
Tel. 952 435 704.
Open year round from 7am till last customer leaves.
Closed Friday.
No credit cards accepted.

Venta El Pozo (The Well) is an old friend. And so is each member of the Guzman family--Felix behind the bar, Dora in the kitchen and son Carlos tending the tables. The family run the place so well, it has become a bench-mark venta against which others may be measured.

Though conveniently located just west of Churriana and easy to get to from anywhere on the Coast, it is at the end of a row of bungalows, with only a small sign. You could easily miss it, so drive slowly and look for an iron gate beneath green vines and pink blossoms from spring to fall.

Entering the spacious patio, you see the well, beautiful if no longer practical, its lip adorned with potted plants, its wrought iron arch entwined with vines. Until recently the patio, which seats around 50, was covered by grape and flowering vines on a wire network. Sadly, the vines got too heavy for safety and had to be removed. They were replaced by colourful shade umbrellas. It's still a delight-ful spot to have lunch.

The large, cool, indoor dining-room, seating some 100 diners, has a zinc-topped bar at which, if you wish, you can lunch well on a large selection of generously sized tapas. Behind the bar is the small but highly productive

kitchen, domain of Dora Guzman and source of world-class bean soups, among many other culinary delights.

The kitchen's best offerings are stews, hotpots, soups and anything else which is cooked low and slow. My prob-here is I am so mad for Dora's spareribs I can rarely be tempted to try something else. If I am, it will usually be the oxtail stew, which is also a pure delight. The portions are large and I reluctantly recommend you restrict your-self to a single dish, starter or main course. If you are still hungry you can always order something else.

The menu, recited by Carlos, depends upon what is available in the market, but always offers a generous choice of fairly standard venta items. The meal of the day, also variable, is inexpensive. The current house wine (it changes periodically) is the acceptable Señorio de Monteviejo, from Valladolíd.

The beautiful overhead vine is gone but the important things remain unchanged. "If El Pozo isn't the perfect venta," I wrote fifteen years ago, "it will certainly do until the real thing comes along." I'll stand by that.

㉕ VENTA EL LIMONAR *

Prolongación Avenida Isaac Peral, s/n, Alhaurín de la Torre.
Telephone 952 414 240.
Open weekdays 7am-11.30pm, weekends 8am-midnight.
No closing day.
Vacation not yet scheduled.
No credit cards accepted.

When El Limonar (The Lemon Grove) opened some nine years ago, it was surrounded by fallow fields. Now, such has been the development around Alhaurín de la Torre, most of those fallow fields have buildings on them. From the venta's veranda, however, one can still see the white-washed walls and the pantiled roof of the old Hacienda de la Victoria, across the road, and the palm trees lining its driveway, even though one has to snap fairly smartly to get a photo between passing vehicles. "Progress is a comfortable disease," as the poet e.e. cummings put it.

And progress proceeds apace at El Limonar. There is a very large dining room under construction at the back of the building and the porch now sports a corrugated tin roof which supplies more than adequate shade for alfresco diners. In fact, the day being warm the last time we went, we opted to have lunch there at one of the 10 widely separated tables. The only drawback is that this area is adjacent to the parking lot.

There is a nice, neat little dining room adjacent to the bar, cool and quiet, with 20 tables or so, if you prefer, but outdoors was apparently the place to be that day, since our fellow diners included owner Rafael Benitez Calderón and members of his family. (I am always reassured to see an owner eating in his own place).

There is a printed menu (in Spanish only) and it is extensive, with 25 to 30 main dishes and a corresponding

number of starters. It includes two main dishes which are
not often seen on venta menus and which are house specialties here: `escalope san jacobo` and *cordon bleu*, both
reasonably priced and highly recommended. The meal of
the day, which one of us had, was perfectly satisfactory: a
good *gazpacho* (with all the gubbins to add), four generous
meatballs, a big salad and a very good *natilla* for the pudding. The price puts this venta comfortably in the inexpensive category. The other meal was the *Cordon Bleu*
(fabulous) with perfectly done chips.

I tend to forget about the bread, or take it for granted,
which is unfair because the bread is so good and produced
in such great variety in Spain. Here, served in mini-
loaves, it is excellent, if you like the kind with a hard,
thick crust.

The house wine, carrying an El Limonar label, is a Don
Darias, which is a cut above most ventas' house wine and
is very reasonably priced. The wine list is modest but does
include all the Faustino reds and the very acceptable
Barbadillo white from Cádiz.

㉖ VENTA ROMERAL DEL ROCIO**

Carretera Churriana-Cártama, Km. 6, Alhaurín de la Torre.
Telephone 952 411 543.
Open from 12 noon to midnight.
No closing day.
Vacation not yet scheduled.
Credit cards: Visa.

Located well out of town, Venta Romeral del Rocio had ample room to spread out...and did so. After you park in the spacious lot, you have a short walk to the entrance. It is cool and dark in this vast interior, which is virtually devoid of natural light. There is room for up to 350 diners, the owner informed us, although only a dozen tables or so are kept set up for drop-in patrons. The bar is part of the dining-room, but is set well off to one side and is not a nuisance to diners.

We took advantage of the full kitchen service from roughly noon to midnight and had the place to ourselves for an early summer lunch. I had a wonderfully tender pork solomillo with a dark, rich pepper sauce which was superb. As is my wont, I asked that the chips be fried "very golden" (*muy doradas*) and they were. They were done exactly how chips should be done but seldom are.

My companion said her chicken breast was grilled to perfection, with a house salad that was supposed to have been for one but which filled a whole dinner plate. The menu is large, with about 20 starters and the same number of quite varied entrées--eight of which are listed as house specialties --so there is plenty of choice.

Although the wine list isn't huge (10 reds, six whites and a couple of rosés) it is interesting and the prices are

right. I opted for a wine I did not know, the Señorio de Irati from Navarra, at only half again as much as the house wine. Since we had been told that both our entrées, though white, were quite rich, I took a chance on the red and was glad I had; it suited admirably.

Romeral del Rocio is the only venta we know that has its own bullring. No serious bullfights are held there, of course, though a variety of other events are. It is next to and visible from another dining- room which can accomodate up to 150. *Flamenco* dancing and other entertainments are regularly scheduled.

The genial owner Amador Soria is devoted to pleasing his customers and welcomes inquiries concerning the schedule of events at the venta, including the summer night barbecues. You may feel free to call him for information, reservations, or to arrange a private party...and you are absolutely not required to participate in a bullfight.

㉗ VENTA EL TINTERO CAMPERO**

Carretera Churriana-Cártama, km.11, Cártama.
No telephone.
Open from 11am till last customer leaves.
No closing day.
Vacation not yet scheduled.
No credit cards accepted.

To use the words "in a class by itself" is terribly tempting because, in a sense, it's true of every venta described in this book, but if the phrase is overused it becomes meaningless. I shall use it only once and right here and now because, if you have never been there before, the odds are that you have never experienced anything like the Venta El Tintero Campero.

It is not its enormous size, though I have seen well over 500 people eating, drinking and having the time of their lives there. Nor is it the quality of the food, though it is good. Rather it is the unique way the place does busines.

On a fine Sunday or holiday, most clients prefer to sit outside on the enormous terrace, under the shade of a high bamboo-and-cloth roof, though you can sit in one of the two big indoor dining-rooms. Wherever you sit, you do not give your complete order to one of the many waiters but, instead, summon any who are carrying plates of whatever it is that strikes your fancy. Each waiter carries as many plates as he can. They circulate inside or out, shouting out their wares.

"Tengo alitas de pollo (I have little chicken wings)", you will hear, or "Coje su gambas rebosadas (get your deep-fried shrimps in batter)". We counted some 25 items thus

offered on our last visit. With more than a dozen waiters circulating at once and crying out their dishes, a group of guitar- playing singers serenading one or another table, and hundreds of customers talking loudly amongst themselves, it is splendidly chaotic. When you're finished, the *cajero* (circulating cashier) counts up the plates (three different prices) and the bottles and charges you accordingly.

The owner – and frequent imposing presence during major meals – is Eduardo "No-No" de la Torres, whose family has owned seven restaurants over the years, the first before 1900. This one and two in Malaga are currently operating. Contrary to our advice on just about every other venta, you want to go to this one on a Sunday or a holiday and enjoy the mayhem.

Eating at El Tintero Campero is an exhilarating experience and is a popular place with foreign residents. We love to take visitors there, most of whom will never forget their visit to a venta which is – no exaggeration – in a class of its own.

㉘ VENTA LA PORRITA*

Plaza Santa Ana, Barriada Acebuchal, Alhaurín de la Torre.
Telephones 952 412 628 & 952 410 595.
Open 9.45am (weekdays 11.30am) till last customer leaves.
Closed Wednesday, weekdays in January.
Closed for vacation second half of September.
Credit Cards: Visa, Mastercharge, American Express.

I recommend Venta La Porrita, owned and operated by
Marco and María García, not because it is my nearest
local, but in spite of it. I already have to write the place off
weekends and holidays from mid-September to May
because there are Malagueños standing in the street waiting to get in. With Wednesday being closing day, I have
to recommend that you go there on Monday, Tuesday or
Thursday. So where does that leave me? I hope not without a table. Well, noblesse oblige and all that.

I will never forget the throat-numbing delight of the
first icy San Miguel I swallowed on those premises one
torrid August afternoon after work 20 years ago. It was a
two-meter-wide-stand-up bar then and I was helping the
crew that was rebuilding the roof on the nearby ruin I had
just rashly purchased.

La Porrita has grown considerably since then and so,
unfortunately, have I. We both take up a lot more room in
the delightful little Plaza Santa Ana than we used to. The
venta has two doors opening directly onto the Plaza. One
leads into a combined bar/dining-room and the other into
a larger, quieter dining area with glass walls, providing a
pleasant view of the tiny park.

The menu, printed in Spanish and flawless English, lists about 40 items plus desserts. There is nothing rare or exclusive to be found, but all standard venta fare is represented, including a variety of pork and veal steaks.

It always hard for me here to choose between the rabbit with garlic or chicken with the same, both served with chips made only in two places – María's kitchen ... and heaven. As usual, the chicken got the call. This may not the best *pollo al ajillo* in Andalusia, but I can't see how any other place could do it better. The trick with the potatoes is to ask for them *muy bien doradas*. My friend had a working man's portion of veal stew over those same superb potatoes, with peas, carrots and a rich gravy. The meal of the day – one of the cheapest you will find anywhere – is on only between 2 and 3pm on weekdays

The Campo Rey house wine, red or white, from Toledo, also among the cheapest to be found, is obviously very basic, but up to the task. The short list permits moving up-market, amongst familiar Riojas, at fair prices.

㉙ TORRE DE VEGA (JUAN'S) *

Plaza Santa Ana, Barriada Acebuchal, Alhaurín de la Torre.
Telephone 952 410 269.
Open year round from 10am to midnight.
Closed Thursday.
No credit cards accepted.

It doesn't seem that long ago that Juan's was just a dirt road bar a short walk from my home. Because the place had a phone, it was known among the area's foreign residents as Juan's Telephone Bar. Some of us still call it that, but whatever you call it, Torre de Vega can only be described as a genuine, black belt Andalusian venta.

The back-to-back bar and kitchen are the living heart of the complex. To get into the place, you must pass through an open-air patio and there you have a choice of sitting in sun or shade. A barbecue grill is set up there in the summer. In the stand-up bar there is a small, fenced off area in which those who like bar chatter and don't mind the Godzilla-sized TV can eat or drink. Beyond the bar is a huge dining-room, mainly used by holiday and special occasion trade, but there are always a few tables set up and you can eat in there, if you like, in quiet solitude. Finally, up on the roof and accessible from the patio, is another area which owner Juan Vega says is "for parties."

Juan's son Marcos and his son-in-law José Antonio are usually behind the bar, waiting tables as required. The kitchen is the domain of Juan's wife, Isobel, a sweet but shy lady who is a wonderful cook. I have eaten *magro con tomate* (pork bits in tomato sauce) all over Spain, including those from my own kitchen, but never better than Isobel's. Gastronomic pleasure is seldom available so cheaply. Juan says that the house specialities are rabbit

and snails, and fine they are. However, a friend from the coast who visits us regularly and frequently eats at Juan's, will have nothing but the *gambas rebosadas* (batter-dipped, deep-fried shrimp) and they are, indeed, plentiful and delicious. Also, for those who like them thoroughly cooked in broth, I recommend the chicken livers. The meal of the day varies with what's on hand and the price, while usually in the cheap category, occasionally gets up into the moderate range. The printed menu is in English as well as in Spanish.

The house wine is one Valdepeñas or another and fairly priced. The list of others features nine Rioja reds, mostly well-known brands at reasonable prices.

Juan still has his telephone and, unlike many bar phones, it has its own little cubicle, where one can converse quietly and privately. It might come in handy for summoning friends to partake of possibly the best *magro con tomate* in all of Andalusia.

㉚ VENTA SEVERINO *

Carretera Coín (A-366), Km. 75, Alhaurín el Grande.
Telephone 952 595 633.
Open from 10am till last customer leaves.
Closed Thursday.
Closes for vacation briefly in summer (variable).
No credit cards accepted.

The main road through "Venta Valley" is the A-366, which is also the main road from the coast to Coín. After Alhaurín de la Torre, the road rises and a couple of the fairways of the new Lauro Golf course appear on the right hand side of the road. Not long after that, the venerable Venta Severino appears.

The new owner Juan Miguél Rueda Conejo grew up on the premises, when his father ran the business from behind the bar. So though he seems young for such responsibility, Juan Miguél has the job well in hand. He greets you and waits on you and is good at both jobs.

Severino is one of those not-too-common ventas which is just about as enjoyable on a horrible, cold, rainy winter day as it is on the balmiest, breeziest summer lunchtime. It's two separate entities, you see. Many's the foul day we've hustled over to Severino in time to get one of the tables near the roaring fire the Ruedas always have going once the weather turns chilly.

The cavernous interior beyond the bar and kitchen is always set up for the management's estimate of how many clients will come in shivering. They have done the best they can with pictures and plants for decoration, but the dining-room is big and, when it's cold outside, nobody

cares about any decoration except that big old fireplace. Our last visit, however, took place in one of the finest early falls we have had in years and we were glad to take advantage of the venta's tin-roofed veranda. As usual, a breeze was blowing through towards the coast and we had the avocado orchard next door for scenery.

The meal of the day is one of the cheapest that exists and I, for one, am totally mystified as to how they do it. What they serve for the main course alone costs more in most places than the entire meal in Severino, and this food is both good and plentiful. There is a very large selection and everything's delicious. There are six acceptable reds on the wine list, four whites and two roses; or you can go with the house Solis, as we did. Whatever you choose will be reasonably priced.

The gradual dwindling in the number of ventas – even over the brief 20 years I have been a patron and observer – is a matter of concern for some of us who believe that they are an important, if not essential, part of Andalusian life. It is gratifying, therefore, to see Venta Severino thriving--and providing the same excellent value for money as ever-- under the direction of a new generation. And, I'm proud to say, it's one of my locals.

㉛ VENTA VAZQUEZ *

Carretera Coín (A-366), Km. 81, Alhaurín de la Torre.
Telephone 952 410 479.
Open from 9.30am to 11pm.
Closed Tuesday.
Vacation not yet scheduled.
No credit cards accepted.

Between kilometres 80 and 81, the Coín Road (A-366) cuts through an old almond grove and there, blocky and not very attractive, sits the Venta Vazquez, doyen of its kind in the Valley of the Ventas. It's right on the road, in the middle of a large lot which provides ample parking, including shade for the lucky owners of eight vehicles.

You climb a dozen steps to get to the action. The large terrace contains 12 tables, with room for plenty more should the need arise. Here, during warm and clement weather, is where you will want to sit. It is cool and breezy here most days, under a high cane ceiling adorned with a flowering vine, with good views of the greater Alhaurín de la Torre countryside. On less pleasant days, or for whatever other reason, you may sit at one of the four or five tables in the spacious bar, which has a fireplace. For the Sunday/holiday throngs, there is a large dining- room with space for 150 patrons or more.

The menu, in Spanish with English translations, offers the usual venta food with two exceptions, kid and *solomillo Iberico*, at about twice the price of the other main dishes. Everything comes with potatoes or vegetables. Roast kid, lamb or suckling pig, must be ordered in advance.

The house wine is that venta favourite, the Peñasol of Felix Solis, from Valdepeñas. The price of the house wine

is lower than at most other ventas. There is also a house Rioja at a very reasonable price, and a few other Riojas.

The meal of the day is good quality and good value. The kid, served stewed, is delicious but it is an annoying mystery to me why this type of meat should be so comparatively expensive – it is, everywhere – in a country where there are so many herds of goats. There is one thing you must know about Venta Vazquez . It serves an excellent pork chop. It's not the size – although they normally come very large – that makes it special, but the tenderness and, especially, the superb flavour.

Also worthy of special mention is Juan, the head – and usually the only – waiter. Though not a member of the family of owner Pedro Vazquez, he has been there for many years. He is efficient and super nice, a model for all venta waiters.

This establishment is a perfect example of what to look for if you are in doubt about the quality of a venta. It has a large parking lot and Spanish patrons of all classes. If you find out that it has been in business forever –and Vazquez has – that clinches it.

㉜ LOS PINOS DEL COTO (Albert's) ***

Cañada de Ceuta, s/n, Churriana.
Telephones 952 435 800 & 952 435 189.
Open from 2 to 4pm and 8 to 11.30 pm (1 to 4pm Sunday).
Closed Monday.
Vacation: closed Mon thru Thurs from January thru March.
Credit cards: Visa, 4B.

The only venta I know that is not Spanish owned and run is Los Pinos del Coto, high up in the Pinos del Coto area of Churriana. Albert Weidig, a German restaurateur, has built here a cozy eating place around a central fireplace and gradually extended it and the adjacent veranda, which commands a breathtaking view of Málaga and the sea over the eerily silent parade of airplanes arriving at and departing from Málaga airport.

I knew Albert in the mid-1980s when he ran a small restaurant called The Little Steps, just off the Plaza San Miguel in Torremolinjos. And when I say "he ran it," I mean just that. Other than a cook, Albert was the staff, the entire staff. In those days, Albert confided that his life's dream was to own his own venta. Well, I watched him make it come true. He was almost the entire staff on that job, too, including carving part of the kitchen out of solid rock with a jackhammer. Twelve years later, he and his wife, Carmen Trueba Prieto, run it with the help of their sons, Erwin and Johann.

The specialities are smoked delights – eight canapes – for starters and pig's knuckle for the main dish. In addition to the usual assortment of soups, salads and *entremeses*, there are some 25 other main dishes on the menu,

which is printed in Spanish, English, Dutch and German. There is only one fish and one chicken dish. Three of us had a tenderloin steak, a small leg of lamb and veal with paprika and red peppers, all highly recommended. Except for homemade mousse and strudel (excellent), the desserts are of the high quality commercial variety.

While not large, the wine list is both unusually good and relatively expensive, for a venta. Apart from the house wines, there are 10 reds (mostly Riojas) compared to just three each of whites and rosés. Two of the reds – a Faustino I *reserva* and a Campillos *gran reserva* are quite expensive, but those are fine wines in most years. We had an Yllera red, a favourite of mine. The house wines are a white and a red El Lugar from Valdepeñas, at close to coast prices, and a Faustino red and a rosé from Rioja.

It is a nice feeling to sit on the veranda and enjoy the wonderful view and to realize that here is a man who deserves his success. In the truest meaning of the phrase, this is The House That Albert Built.

㉝ VENTA LOS CABALES*

Carretera Coín-Cártama (A-355), Km. 3+, Cártama.
Telephone 952 420 091.
Open from 8am to 11pm.
Closed Monday.
Vacation not yet scheduled
No credit cards accepted

Los Cabales, owned and run by the Morales Perez family, has been open since 1989, but until quite recently you might have zipped right by it, tucked as it is in the pocket of a sharp turn on a little-used road, the A-355. There is no chance of that now since the addition of an eye-catching green and white striped awning over the entrance.

 You enter a large dining--room with windows on three sides, though frankly there's not much to look out upon. This room is designed to accommodate Sunday/holiday/ first communion crowds and could easily hold 200 people. During the week, however, only a dozen or so tables are set up, with red-and-white-checked tablecloths, for those who enjoy the bright spaciousness of the big room. The main decorations are green plants atop old wine barrels.

 Passing into the bar area, you will find a small dining-room on your left with seven tables for four and another on your right with one large and two small tables. Tile wainscoting, ceiling fans, electrified candle sconces, wine racks and an assortment of framed pictures create a pleasant atmosphere. The classic zinc bar has stools, but even when busy it isn't a bother to diners. It and all the necessary utilities – public telephone, commercial desserts cooler, toilets etc.--are screened off from diners by a lattice divider. Moldings around the fans, the sconces and the bar ceiling add a touch of class.

You will not be shown a printed menu but, if you ask, you will be told--probably by waiter Antonio, son of chef Antonio-that lamb, done in various ways, is the house speciality. I have had it roasted and pronounce it good. It is, however, heavy for lunch and relatively expensive. The meal of the day, on the other hand, is a wonder.

In a recent sitting, *pipirrana* (chopped veg salad, here including seafood), selected as the starter, was not only full of shellfish, it was a small meal in itself. The main course, four large slices of fresh tuna cooked in an onion sauce and served with pilaf rice and *patatas a lo pobre* (home-fried potatoes), was as good as it was huge. With a choice of simple desserts and half a bottle of the house wine (Viña del Lagar, from Valdepeñas), this meal was an incredible bargain at about half the price of the lamb.

Because they are more intimate and very nicely decorated with tables and seat cushions covered with brightly woven material from the Alpujarras, we prefer to eat in either of the two dining areas near the bar. Since these areas contain a total of only 10 tables, however, we suggest that you plan to have lunch early – say between 1 and 2pm – especially if it is a nice day.

㉞ VENTA LOS ARCOS*

Carretera Coín-Cártama (A-355), Km. 5+, Alhaurín el Grande.
Telephone 952 112 590.
Open from 9am to 10pm in winter, later in summer.
Closed Thursday.
Vacation usually taken in June.
No credit cards accepted.

I first visited Los Arcos in 1982, when the venta and I were both completing our first year of life in Spain. I did not know it at the time, but I was one of its first customers. That I am still a customer surely says something about the place.

I still prefer to eat in the relatively small dining-room beside the bar – it's normally set up for 40 to 50 customers – in which one is comfortable summer (a/c) or winter (fireplace). It is cheek by jowl with the large, zinc-topped bar, but that popular feature is thoughtfully screened off from the dining room and, in my experience, does not bother diners, noisewise.

Others may prefer the old open-air terrace – now enlarged to accommodate at least a hundred people and closed in as well as nicely decorated with wagon wheel chandeliers, oversized Spanish fans and assorted greenery – or the shaded outside area with apparent unlimited capacity to expand. The large dining-room downstairs may be booked for private parties.

Arcos is a friendly place which is popular with foreigners and Spaniards. The high quality meal of the day– well inside our least expensive category – is certainly one of the reasons why. On our last visit, my companion enthused over her selected starter, the so-called vegetable soup, which was in reality a mystery purée containing pieces of potatoes, string beans, chickpeas and a large

piece of sausage. Her main dish was a large portion of fried *boquerones* accompanied by a good house salad. She couldn't even think about tackling one of the standard desserts offered.

Waiter Juan Luís, named after his father, owner Juan Luís Lucena , has been working in the venta since he was 13 and is now 30. He advised us that there were two specials that day that were not on the menu, fresh salmon and fresh tuna. I had the latter, two steaks served in a tomato sauce with an excellent salad and chips properly done. It was a big, fine meal, and very reasonably priced.

The menu is extensive – 16 *carnes a la brasa* alone – with all the things usually found on venta menus and a number of uncommon ones, like *jibia*. The bread, a dark beige colour, is excellent if, like me, you like yours heavy textured and hard-crusted.

The house wine is the popular Valdepeñas Viña del Lugar. The list is short (10 reds, five whites, three rosés and four *cavas*) but adequate. The super salesman from Faustino who covers this area has struck again, with half the offerings being supplied by his employer. There's a decent Marqués de Cáceres there as well.

㉟ VENTA PLATERO *

Carretera Coín-Cártama (A-355), Km. 3.5, Coín.
Telephones 952 452 934 & 952 450 716.
Open from 9am till last customer leaves.
Closed Wednesday.
Vacation taken when no big events are booked.
No credit cards accepted.

We've been going to the Venta Platero regularly since it was opened by the Luna family in 1990. Very little has changed since then, including the prices.

The dining-room shares a wall with the separate bar and on that wall is one of those big, idyllic pictures you stick up like wallpaper. This one shows an alpine lake as seen through a 16-pane window. It can be quite mesmerizing while you wait to place your order. The other three walls are made up of sliding glass panels and customers, as well as staff, open and close them at will.Outside, the parking lot is dotted with young olive trees, which means some lucky customers get to park their cars in the shade.

Platero has a system – unique in our experience, outside of Chinese restaurants – which we find very satisfying. You can have a *ración* (portion) of most items on the menu or a *media ración*, a half portion which fills a bread plate. So, if everyone orders something different, everyone gets to try a little of everything.

Not only does this venta have a superb kitchen, it seems to be committed to keeping prices down as well. There were five in our party and we each had ample shares of

deep-fried anchovies, breaded bass, rabbit in garlic, pork on skewers, ribs, mixed salad, two bottles of house wine and either home-made or fancy commercial dessert for a cost to each of us of an inexpensive meal of the day.

The Viña del Lugar house wine, red and white, is adequate and the cheapest we have yet found, but there is a short wine list (only eight reds, two whites and a rosé) which will permit you to go slightly upmarket.

A separate building behind the dining-room is a vast venue for special events which seats up to 500 people. It is awesome.

As we often did in writing this book, we had a late lunch. We found that if we went early there was always the chance that the place would still be bustling when we finished, and the people we needed to answer our questions might have been too busy with other customers. This time was a busy day and, though we got the information we needed, we had to wait for several big trucks to pull out before we could take some pictures. It says something about Platero that the trucks were from all over – local delivery vans and big 18-wheelers with license plates from hundreds of kilometers away.

㊱ VENTA LAS PALMERAS ✳✳✳

Carretera Alhaurín El Grande–Coin (A–366), Km. 64, Coin.
Telephone 952 451 364.
Open year round from 1 to 5pm.
Closed Wednesday.
No credit cards accepted.

To many people, Las Palmeras looks exactly as a venta should. The old house is set back from the road and is scarcely noticed, once the car is parked. It is the garden, where customers eat, which draws the attention like fresh blossoms draw honey bees.

The first thing you are aware of approaching the place from either direction is the group of some half dozen magnificent old date-bearing palms with their huge umbrella crowns of pinnate fronds that shade the 20 or so tables set up for diners in the garden.

Entering the garden, you are awed by the canopy of wisteria vines, which are supported on a network of wires and shade many of the tables. With the *aljibe*, the open water reservoir, in the background, the overall effect is like being in an oasis, especially on a hot summer day. Diners can move indoors in winter.

There is no meal of the day on the printed menu, so we put together one of our own, consisting of salad, a cheap-but-good main dish, a half bottle of the house red, bread and fruit for dessert.

Stewed rabbit with garlic is one of the five specialities here and it is one of the dishes venta cognoscenti will recommend at Las Palmeras, though we thought another of

the specialities, *lomo con patatas fritas* (pork loin with chips) was better. The quite inexpensive meatballs and the fried peppers were good. There is a good choice of food here – 15 soups, salads and miscellaneous starters, 10 main dishes and a dozen or so of the usual venta desserts, including whatever fruit is in season.

On our last visit, the house wine was called Castillo de Monteros. It was disappointing and overpriced. I recommend you take your choice instead from a not terribly distinguished list – five reds and five whites – which are drinkable if rather pricey.

Maybe there are ventas in this book that serve better food than at Las Palmeras, but if you take those majestic palms and restful, shady ambience into account...well, there are certainly worse ways – and places – to spend a couple of hours over lunch.

㊲ VENTA LOS MORENOS **

Carretera Alhaurín el Grande–Mijas (A-387), Km. 4,
Alhaurín el Grande.
Telephone 95 249 1193.
Open year round from 10am till last customer leaves.
Closed Thursday.
Credit cards: Visa, Mastercard, Eurocard.

Los Morenos is one of the oldest and most popular of the
ventas on the outskirts of three different municipalities:
Mijas, Coín and Alhaurín el Grande. In fact, located at
the new traffic circle where roads A-387 and MA-426
meet, it is officially situated in Alhaurín. The location is
so perfect that if ventas did not exist, someone would have
to invent the first one and put it right there.
Unquestionably "out in the country," it is an easy drive
from almost anywhere on the middle Costa del Sol or adjacent inland environments. If you are a regular, sooner or
later you'll meet everyone you know at Los Morenos.

At the core of the complex is an intimate bar with a
small lounge, neither of which are any nuisance to diners.
In front is the large, open terrace, so surrounded by greenery, inside and out, that it's like a garden and the cane roof
is so high you expect to look up and see clouds. This is the
dining area that gets most of the action. Behind the bar
and lounge is a large room, with a big fireplace. The walls
are adorned with the oil paintings of an artist who lives
nearby and you can buy on the spot any which are not
already sold. You can eat in here whenever you wish, but
it is mainly used for large groups celebrating such occasions as first communions. Behind this room is the large,
completely open terrace.

The menu is the size of a tabloid newspaper and offers many delights: four soups, three salads, three *tortillas* and several other starters, a dozen fish and more than 20 meat entrees and 15 or so desserts. The specialties, however, are the various *carnes a la brasa*. The barbecued spareribs, served so many ways in Spain, are here cooked American style, each rib (or a pair, if small) cut from the rack and cooked, with basting sauce, on a grill, over charcoal. Exquisite...and so cheap you won't believe it. Meal of the day is at the bottom of our medium-priced category. The house wine is the perfectly adequate Viña de Lugar, but there is a good list of Riojas, if you are feeling expansive.

Owner Juan Moreno tends the bar. His father, now deceased, opened the place in 1970. Juan is pleased that his business has prospered over the years and is grateful to the near-even split of Spanish and foreign customers who have supported it in ever-increasing numbers. One price he has paid, however, is that in 27 years he hasn't been able to find time to take a vacation. He tried it last year and it didn't work out. That's the trouble with doing things right: people never leave you alone.

㊳ VENTA LOS CONDES *

Carretera Mijas-Coín (A-387), Km. 8, Valtocado, Mijas.
Telephone 952 485 714.
Open year round from 7am till last customer leaves.
No closing day.
No credit cards accepted.

Seeing Los Condes back in action was like going to a class reunion and meeting old friends. Ten or 12 years ago, we used to regularly travel the Mijas-Coín road and would occasionally stop at the tiny venta. We weren't exactly regulars, but we enjoyed the friendly intimacy of the place. Then one day the venta was closed. The facade remained the same and the signboard stayed in place. It was simply no longer in business. Now, just as unexpectedly, it's open again.

One big advantage the new owner José Antonio Gonzalez has over his predecessors is the development of the vast residential area of Valtocado, one entrance of which is right across the road. This means not only custom from the new residents, but also from construction workers. On recent visits, we have seen plenty of both.

On working days, the choice is between sitting at the large bar or in the adjacent, glassed-in, cane-ceilinged veranda, which seats 35 to 40 customers. From some of the veranda tables, part of the pine forest above and behind the venta can be seen. For Sundays, holidays and special occasions, there is a nicely decorated, blue and white dining-room upstairs which seats about 60 patrons.

The menu, printed in Spanish and English, is fairly short but covers just about all basic venta items plus a

couple of exotic ones, such as sole, swordfish and *paella*. The house has not decided on specialties as yet, so we went somewhat above the average price (which still wasn't very expensive) and had *solomillos de cerdo*, one grilled and one with pepper sauce. Both were very good and are recommended. The cost of the meal of the day is well below the top of the inexpensive category.

The wine situation at Los Condes when we were there last fall was, ah, somewhat fluid. We asked for the house red and were served a Concejal *crianza* 1993 from Valdepeñas, which was satisfying and the price was right There was, however, no wine list and even if there had been, it would have been extremely short. There was a rack in the bar containing a few Riojas – Marques de Riscal, Marques de Caceres, Faustino, Campo Viejo, Siglo and Romeral – and, if you didn't want the Concejal, it was from there that you had to make your choice.

㊴ VENTA SIERRA MIJAS *

Carretera de Circunvalacíon de Mijas (A-387), Km. 12, Mijas.
Telephone 952 486 286.
Open year round from 9am till last customer leaves.
No closing day.
Credit cards: Servired, Eurocard, Mastercard, Visa.

Venta Sierra Mijas owner Miguel Angel García admits
he's not an architect or builder but he adds with quiet
pride, "I designed this place and laid many of its bricks."
Indeed, he wasn't a restaurateur either until 1996, when he
abandoned the discotheque business to launch his venta.

He admits he is still learning the business, but says he
personally tests everything that comes out of the kitchen,
listens to the suggestions of his clientele, and tries to give
them what they want. For example, garlic bread is standard, at the same charge as regular bread, because a number of his foreign customers wanted it. At the time we
were there, the menu was undergoing a complete revision.

The menu of the day falls into our inexpensive category and offers a good selection of standard items, but there
is another "special" menu at a set price featuring more
upmarket selections for twice the price of the meal of the
day. We knew we would have to try at least one *paella* for
this book but had been putting it off because normally it
is served for a minimum of two people, limiting our tast-
ing capacity.

Since a British house guest was assisting us with our
enquiries, this seemed like a good time. It was not the

best *paella* I have ever eaten (that was in Valencia) but it was good, ample and contained all the right ingredients. Our friend said his stuffed peppers Navarra was as good a meal as he had had on several visits to ventas with us.

The house wine, Vino Ropany from La Mancha, is a little pricey but perfectly adequate. One thing led to another and we also tried a red, the Castillo Irache 1985 Reserva from Navarra, almost twice the price as the Ropany, but a very nice wine and a better buy. Because of the menu revision, there was no printed wine list, but the owner assured us that it will be representative.

Sierra Mijas is perched above Mijas on the by–pass and has a panoramic view over the pueblo to Fuengirola and the coast. Tall eucalyptus and pine trees shade the seven tables on the lower terrace. There are also a few tables beside the road, actually on the bar roof, from where the view is even more stunning. With such views, I would have accepted a meal of far lesser quality.

⑳ VENTA LA TORRE *

Carretera Vieja Mijas Costa-Coín (MA-426), Km. 5, Mijas Costa.
Telephone 952 461 545.
Open year round from 1 to 5pm and 7 to 11pm.
Closed Saturday.
Credit card: Visa, Mastercard, Eurocard, Maestra, Telepago.

I remember when there seemed to be more ventas near Mijas Golf than there were holes on the club's two courses. No more. Of the surviving four eating places within a drive and a chip shot of the entrance, two are now restaurants and one is a *meson*. Only La Torre still proclaims itself — and with pride – as a venta.

This is one of the greybeards of the ventas located in the middle of the Costa del Sol, in business for 30 years and with a long roster of regular patrons...and not just golfers. Señor Diaz Porras, the owner, has recently carried out major revisions, inside and out, and the building looks smarter than ever, with three large bucolic scenes fashioned from ceramic tile set into the roadside facade.

You enter through an enclosed veranda seating perhaps 50 customers and enter an intimate, climate-controlled bar, which is where most of the regulars hang. If that is where you want to have lunch, go early, because seating is limited. Last time around we arrived a bit late and the bar tables were all taken.

We decided to eat in the large dining-room beyond the bar, with the workers. The large dining-room in any venta near a construction site is usually full of workers between

2 and 3pm and we occasionally like to eat with them for a change in pace and atmosphere.

Because we are used to it, we weren't surprised to find a bottle of the red house wine, ice cold (it was summer), on the table, with a large bottle of Casera, also cold. You don't have to have this if you don't want it and, indeed, that was our waiter's first question. Since we had elected to chow down with the troops that day, we said "*Si*." I suspect that the workers get a very special rate on the meal of the day, which is fine. After all, it's for them that it exists. Of course, you can order whatever you want, no matter where you sit

The meal of the day was quite cheap, as was my companion's chicken, served with the ubiquitous chips. My *rabo de toro* (oxtail stew) was considerably more, but still fairly priced. The house wine, Viña Perea from Ciudad Real, was drinkable but, in all honesty, better with the Casera than without. The wine list contains a couple of pricey numbers, but a reasonable selection of not terribly distinguished others at standard prices.

⑪ VENTA EL JINETE **

Carretera Cala Golf, Km. 4, Mijas Costa.
Telephone 95 211 9170.
Open year round from 11am to 11pm.
No closing day.
Credit cards: Visa, Mastercard, Eurocard .

Searching for a venta at the height of the tourist season, we found ourselves trapped in the notorious summer traffic on the N-340. After an hour of bumper-to-bumper torture, we gave up and got off at the Cala de Mijas, hoping we could circumnavigate the golf course via goat tracks and dry river beds and eventually reach our home in Alhaurín de la Torre.

Cruising effortlessly down the new, private road to La Cala Golf, the last thing I expected to see was a venta. But there it was, El Jinete, sitting just high enough above and far enough back from the road to create the impression that it is much smaller than it is.

There are 15 or 16 tables on the covered veranda where we had lunch, with room for more if need be. The ceiling is of cane and around its edges are hung clear plastic bags filled with water, an Andalusian custom for discouraging flies. It sounds weird, I know, but it seems to work, otherwise we would surely have been bothered by the pests from the nearby stable which gives the venta its name.

Inside is a six-stool, zinc-topped bar at which I would surely hang out occasionally if I lived in the neighborhood, and booths or tables for another 50 or 60 diners. Owner Rafael Cabrera Cano, who was tending bar when we were

there, told us that the place has been in business since 1993 and that his regulars are mainly local non-Spanish residents.

The printed menu is in Spanish, English and German but I put it aside when the waiter told me the barbecue grill provided the house specialities. I not only love ribs, I also reckon they're a good test of a barbecuer's expertise. Served with a baked potato with *alioli* and half a grilled tomato, the three large ones I had passed the test easily.

Jinete does not offer a meal of the day and putting together one from the cheaper dishes, as we did, sent the price up well into the medium range, but the meal (*gazpacho*, pork brochette and *flan*) could not be faulted.

The house wine was Don Opas from Valdepeñas and, if not something you want to buy by the case, got the job done and was cheap enough. The wine list is short but provocative and what is offered is very fairly priced.

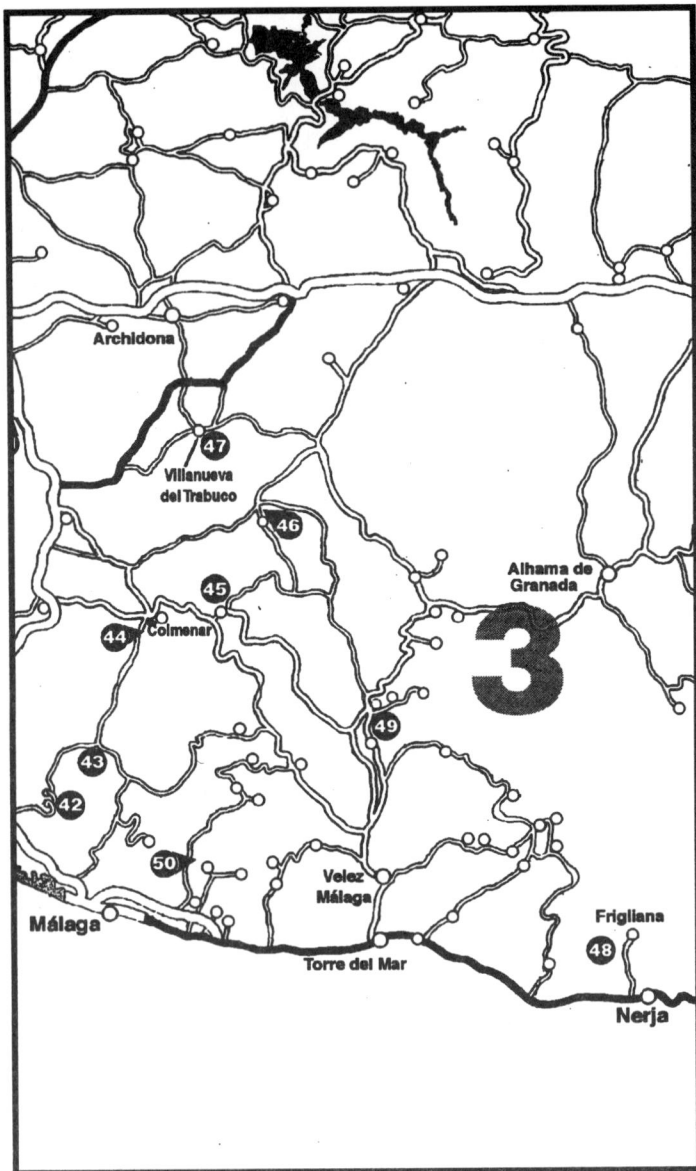

VENTAS MAP 3   PAGE

㊷ VENTA LOS OLIVOS **

Carretera Malaga-Colmenar (C-345), Km. 555, Málaga.
Telephone 952 269 958.
Open year round from 12noon till last customer leaves.
No closing day.
No credit cards accepted.

Amongst the cluster of ventas near Málaga, Los Olivos stands above the rest. I mean literally. There is a sign on the road but you cannot see the venta. When the building finally comes into view, at the end of a rough driveway, it seems tiny. It is not.

You pass a few tables sitting in the sun and enter the first dining- room, mostly employed to catch the overflow of holiday crowds. Beyond is the main dining-room, normally seating about 120 patrons but with room for at least a dozen more tables if needed. There is a small stand-up bar in the corner by the kitchen. Beyond the large windows at the back of this room, and down a few steps, is a big open-air patio, some of it under shade cover, which will easily accommodate 200 customers or more. It is from the rear of the main dining-room and from the patio that the big advantage which Olivos has over its neighbours is apparent – the views, especially of the city of Málaga.

Except for those views, Los Olivos is not a place you will remember because of its physical beauty. It's just a couple of big rooms and a sprawling deck. The food, however, is good and cheap, for what it is. The specialities are wild boar and venison and the latter is only available in season, meaning fall and winter. Having just had boar elsewhere, I asked about other, tamer specialities and Reme, the waitress and daughter of the García Barbas family who lease the place, recommended the *cordero a la pastoril* (lamb, shepherd's style). With lots of chopped lamb

pieces cooked with almonds in a light sauce, it was delicious. Others present had the sea bass (excellent, ample serving), pork loin steak (big, "very good") and ribs (unusual in that the large, fatty pieces were not attached to rib bones, but were very flavourful). There was no meal of the day and the one we figured out took the price to near the top of our medium-priced menu.

There are two house wines. One is meant to be drunk with Casera, the other is Avadon, from Rioja, and is adequate. We had a Faustino VII at a fair price and it was acceptable. The list is large, with a wide price range.

There is no easy way to get to Los Olivos. One way is to go into the centre of Malaga, get on Calle Victoria and follow the signs marked Granada/Cordoba/Sevilla until you come to the first of the signs pointing to Colmenar, which you then follow. The other is to belt on up the main road north (N-331) until you get to the first Colmenar exit and follow your nose back down to Málaga on the C-345. Either way, you will be glad you took the trouble...provided you don't go on Sunday or a holiday.

㊸ VENTA GALWEY **

Carretera de los Montes (C-345), Km. 544, Málaga.
Telephone 952 110 128.
Open year round from 9am to midnight.
No closing day.
No credit cards accepted

The outside of this venta is pretty much of a car-stopper
on a summer's day – an old, whitewashed building with a
few tables sitting under the shade of a flowering vine.
Inside, one after another, are three long, narrow dining
rooms, with an open terrace beyond the last of them overlooking the Mountains of Malaga.

On your left as you enter is a bar extending across one
end of rooms one and two. Room one has a fireplace,
which probably means that it is the centre of winter activ-
ity, but it is room two which, in addition to the terrace, is
set up for weekday trade in the summer. It is attractive,
with tile wainscoting, beamed ceiling, wagon wheel chandeliers and farm and kitchen artifacts on the walls.

One of our group had the "mountain plate," typical of
the area and a lot of food for a small price. Another had
the kid with almonds, a gourmet item among standard
venta offerings, we all agreed, and fairly priced. There
being no meal of the day on offer, my usual companion had
a leg joint of chicken which she found tender and tasty
and, as is not always the case, delicately flavoured with
the garlic and onion with which it was cooked.

To my surprise, one of the two advertised house specialties, wild boar, was available, though it was then mid-

summer. Presumably, it was frozen but that did not diminish its flavour. It was served it to me in a rich stew with myriad almonds, another generous gourmet treat and offered at no more than half what one would expect to pay in a conventional restaurant on the coast. Our constructed meal of the day, as usual, puts the venta in the medium-priced category.

The wine list is not only surprisingly large for a venta (about 35 items), but has several prestigious wines running well up into the thousands of pesetas per bottle. In this venta, as in many others, there are two house wines, one Rioja and one not. Unless you want to drink your wine with a mixer, you want the Rioja. The Rioja house wine here was Avadon, unknown to me but adequate.

Our waiter, Antonio, son of the García Barbas family which owns Galwey, told us the building had been there since the 15th century and we read in a guidebook later that it had been named after an English traveller.

㊹ VENTA LOS ARRIEROS *

HOTEL DE MONTAÑA
Carretera Casabermeja-Colmenar (A-355) , Km. 8, Colmenar.
Telephone 952 730 352 or 952 731 066.
Open year round during normal dining hours (bar open all day).
No closing day.
Credit cards: Visa, Mastercard, Eurocard.

This was a first for us and a unique combination – a bona fide venta combined with a country hotel. The venta came first, in 1988, and in 1994 it was expanded to incorporate a 14-room, one-star hotel.

At first sight, the building is awesome. You are negotiating the twisting, uphill road to Colmenar when you round a bend and there stands what appears to be the ancestral home of Thomas Jefferson. Following the shock of encountering the totally unexpected, you will probably need something to steady your nerves, and will find it to your right the instant you step through the front door. It is an attractive bar which someone worked hard to make that way. Serrano hams and strings of garlic and peppers hang from the ceiling, along with dozens of straw-covered bottles. Wine is displayed on several wall racks and three large barrels, dated 1915, are stacked in a corner. A chilled *fino* (dry sherry) tastes better, somehow, in such a setting; the second one even more so.

A very large dining-room, only partially set up for daily trade and nicely decorated with prints and various artifacts, is immediately adjacent to the bar. There you may enjoy "homemade specialties typical of Axarquia," we were informed by our waiter, a member of the Sanchez Palumbo family which owns the business. Among those we were

pleased to try were the *porra antequerrana* (a very thick gazpacho with egg and meat bits on the side) and *carne mechada* (here, very thin slices of pork in brown gravy). We were given a price for a meal of the day which would put it in our cheapest category but, for reasons we were unable to comprehend, the kitchen couldn't produce one just then.

The wine list, containing about a dozen Riojas, isn't bad, but the offerings are a bit pricey, though we found the white wine of the house (Guerola, from Valdepeñas) to be quite adequate and fairly priced.

The two bedrooms we looked at had air conditioning, television and good pastoral views. They were both immaculate and very reasonably priced. The Hotel Montaña presents one of those get-away opportunities to take a break from the hustle and bustle of the "Costa" and spend a night or two in rural Andalusia in a pretty little country inn. When there's a genuine Spanish venta on the premises, it's just about irresistible.

㊺ VENTA SAN MIGUEL **

Carretera C-340, Alfarnatejo.
Telephone 952 111 742
Open year round from 9am till last customer leaves.
No closing day.
No credit cards accepted.

If, like us, you have driven all over the twisting roads of northern Axarquía, enjoying the views of the austere mountains, the lovely reservoir and the myriad tiny villages, you might drive right by the Venta San Miguel without a second thought. If it's anywhere near mealtime, that would be a big mistake. True, it doesn't bear much resemblance to a Frank Lloyd Wright design and the only view is from the veranda to some olive trees across the street, but owner, cook and waitress Francisca Jimenez will give you a big smile and the best home-built lasagna you are likely to find this side of the Italian Piedmonte.

To get to the dining-room, you pass through the glassed-in veranda – glass out for the summer – and the little stand-up bar, supervised by Francisca's husband, Miguel. It is he, by the way, together with Francisca's brother and her first son, whose given names led them to name the venta after that particular saint.

My companion had the lasagna and I had the grilled quail, and we both had *patatas a lo pobre* (skillet-fried sliced potatoes, not chips) and agreed they were as good as we've ever had them. Then we each had desserts made on the premises: *flan* (you all know what that is) and *leche frita* ("fried milk", which seems to be little cinnamon donuts made out of custard). We were two happy campers.

We had asked about the fixed price meal of the day, but Francisca just pointed at the price list and shrugged, clearly wondering why a fixed price meal would be a concern when prices are that low. Understandable enough, but when one adds up the cheapest items on this menu – or practically that of any other venta – the total gets up over the top of our cheapest category. The wine list was short and we had the usual Soldepeñas.

When we arrived, a group of old men had command of a corner of the veranda and were playing one of those cabalistic Spanish card games. Francisca said they were regular customers and some even came regularly from Fuengirola. With every shortcut, the closest Fuengirola can be to Venta San Miguel is a 150-kilometer round trip. I guess we aren't the only ones who like Francisca's *patatas a lo pobre*.

㊻ ANTIGUA VENTA DE ALFARNATE ***

Carretera Vieja Málaga-Granada (MA-115), Km. 513, Alfarnate.
Telephone 952 759 235.

**Before going to press, we learned that this venta was
being renovated and would not be reopened until this
coming 1998 winter season. We decided to keep it in the
book because it is such an outstanding venta. You should
call (maybe from October onwards) before making the
trip. If you should arrive there to find it still closed, you
could return to the old Málaga-Granada road and drive
down the Carretera 345 to Venta Galwey (see page 106).**

To visit the Antigua Venta de Alfarnate is to literally take
a trip into Spain's past. The title deed to the building is
dated 1691, but the history of the establishment as an eating place can be traced back, with reasonable reliability, to
the 13th century. Fittingly, it is located on a piece of one
of the oldest roads in the province.

To get there, take N-331, the main road north from
Malaga, turn off at the first Colmenar exit and bear right.
Turn left on C-340 and, very soon, right on MA-115. From
there on cruise through hill country peppered with olive
and almond trees and offering bucolic views in all directions. Even at sightseer's speed, you will soon come upon
the solitary whitewashed building, with its roof of multi-
colored pantiles and its name modestly displayed in small
green and white ceramic tiles set into the wall.

The door opens into the picturesque bar with a low, log-
beamed ceiling and a fireplace. The walls are adorned
with old paintings and bullfight posters, copper utensils,
and other memorabilia from a Spain that is no more. Six

tables for four do not crowd the room. The service bar is unobtrusive. To the right of the entry door is the principal dining- room, set up for about 40 diners.

The food is country-hearty. The house speciality *huevos a la bestia* – also designated as "the meal of the day" – is gargantuan. Meat, sausage, eggs, veg, on a bed of *migas*, all served in a bowl the size of a crash helmet. It is splendid, but it is a meal for a genuine trencherman and it is not easily divided. Also, it is the most expensive meal of the day we have found in any venta. Unless you are very hungry, try instead the magnificent *jamon asado al vino de los montes*. And someone else please have the *berenjenas con miel de caña* (eggplant fritters deep-fried in honey batter). They give you enough of them for a generous meal, or you can share them with your companions.

The wine list is short and relatively expensive. Go with the *vino de monte*. It's white but it goes with everything, but take care because indiscriminate consumption will unravel your socks.

ⓐ VENTA TALILLAS *

Avenida Antoñico Rosa, Villanueva del Trabuco.
Telephone 952 751 895.
Open year round from 9am till last customer leaves.
No closing day.
Credit cards: Visa, Unicaja .

There are two problems you face when you decide to have a meal at Venta Talillas. The first is finding it. We did so quite by accident, when we were looking for another place. Here's how to get there (because this is a place you won't want to miss). Take the Málaga ring road (N-340) and the branch to Antequera (N-331) when you come to it. Where the road splits again, take A-359 to Granada. Take any of the three exits to Villanueva del Trabuco. In that small town, all you have to do is drive around until you see one of the arrow-shaped signs cleverly installed here and there by Antonio Pascual Valencia, the owner of Venta Talillas. Those little signs will unerringly lead you there.

What you see when you finally find it is a plain square building sitting on its own in the middle of a large parking lot. Across its front is a big terrace with a retractable awning. In the summer this terrace is filled with tables. Behind the building is a children's playground and covered parking for about 20 cars.

Whatever your business, you enter by the same door. The bar is on your left, the working day dining-room on your right, with a discreet lattice screen between the two. We were waited on by the affable Antonio himself, who explained that not everything on the enormous menu was available every day, though he gave us a large selection of items to make up a meal of the day, which falls into our

114

inexpensive category. He had no idea who we were, but he very graciously set out bowls of olives and *setas* (wild mushrooms*),* on the house.

There were four of us and we all tried different things, swapping tastes like judges at a cooking competition. What we liked best were the *setas*, the *porra antequerana*, the *picadillo*, the *sopa de mariscos*, the *churrasco* (one of the house specialties) and the *flan*.

The small wine list contains some dozen choices, all familiar and more than fairly priced, but we were well-satisfied with the ultra-cheap house wine, Condestable from Jumilla, and available in three colours.

The second problem – referred to in the opening sentence – is coping with the enormous amounts of food which the good Talillas family keeps bringing to your table. Not eating for several days before your visit is a solution, but not very practical. Skipping dessert helps a bit, but not when I tell you that this is the best *flan* we had in any venta and the only one which I believe, without question, was made from scratch in the venta kitchen. When the food is this good, what's another few ounces?

㊽ VENTA EL CORTIJO **

Carretera Frigiliana-Torrox, Km. 4, Frigiliana.
Telephone 952 115 727.
Open year round from 11.30am till last customer leaves.
No closing day.
Credit cards: Visa, Unicaja, Tarjeta 6,000.

Just five kilometres due north of the bustling seaside town of Nerja is the picture-postcard village of Frigiliana, whose civic leaders have done a commendable job of preventing it from becoming just another tourist trap. With the new ring road around Malaga, the area is a rewarding focal point for a day trip from as far away as Estepona.

Of course, there are many places to eat in a tourist area like this. We checked out all the ventas we could find, at least cursorily, and asked for local recommendations. Based on the data received, we chose Venta El Cortijo – and didn't regret it.

It's past Frigiliana on the road to Torrox, in the foothills of the Sierra de Enmedio. The entry is through an intimate bar between the kitchen and the dining-room. There are six tables there, but we preferred the brighter main dining-room with its views of the mountain valley and, on a clear day, the sea. On the other side of the glass wall is an open terrace for 30 patrons, under sun umbrellas.

José Antonio Rodriguez has owned the place for three years. According to his daughter, the beautifully-named Coral, everything on the 25-item menu is a house speciality. I love *gambas pil-pil* (shrimp in hot, spicy oil), an item not always offered in ventas, so when I saw it here, it was my choice. It was served as it should be with the oil bubbling

If, as I do, you mop up the oil with your bread, this dish can make a satisfying meal all by itself.

There is no official meal of the day and the one my companion constructed – lentil soup loaded with meat and veg, *cerdo con pisto* (pork pieces with mixed vegetables in a sort of stew) and a glass of the local wine – added up to the middle price range. It was good...and a lot of food. The house wine was Soldepeñas, but the wines on the small list were inexpensive, so I went with the Tres Ducados white from Bodegas Campo Viejo and was well satisfied.

Since you have come this far – and assuming it's a clear day – I recommend that you go forward, rather than back, to the town of Torrox and thence to the N-340. It's not pedal-to-the-metal driving, but the mountain scenery is enjoyable. Back on the N-340 you will have to put up with some stop-and-go traffic, but you can cut up to the new bypass near Algarrobo. Meanwhile, you can think about the good meal you had at El Cortijo, where everything on

❹ VENTA BAR ZALIA ✱✱✱

Puente Don Manuel 5, Alcaucín.
Telephones 989 778 739 and 989 251 0836.
Open from 10.30am to 11pm (later in summer).
Closed for vacation irregularly in winter (call before going).
No credit cards accepted.

Sad to say, not everyone who deals with the public is good at it. José Manuel Martín, who took over from his father at the Venta Bar Zalia, is very good at it. He takes pride in his work but doesn't let being efficient get in the way of being pleasant. We have had at least civil treatment in every venta mentioned in this book, but José is the only individual who ever came to our table twice during the course of a meal, once to ask if we were happy with the wine and again to find out if our food was satisfactory.

And very satisfactory everything was. I had one of the two house specialities, stewed goat, and my companion had a generous *tapa* of the other speciality, *callos,* followed by *filetillas de cerdo.* The wine was a young, very reasonably priced Heredad de Altillo Rioja red. My goat was tender and delicate, and my friend said the *callos* and the little pork filets were delicious.

We were looking for another place when we turned off the A–335 onto MA–128 and immediately on our left we saw Venta Zalia. We figured that any place bold enough to announce its presence in green block letters four feet high on its facade wasn't ashamed of what it had to offer, so we pulled into the 15-car parking lot.

Beyond a tin-roofed veranda with five tables, we entered a good-sized room exuding a feeling of welcome. On the right was a U-shaped, zinc-topped bar with some

dozen stools. Above it hung *serrano* hams for sale. On the left was a dining area with five round tables, each with four straw-bottomed chairs, all painted green and decorated with white flowers. The wallls were hung with ceramic plates and brass and copper kitchen implements.

The menu (there is one in Spanish and another in English and German) is more than adequate with about 15 main courses in the standard venta price range and another six more upmarket, such as steaks and my goat dish.The house wine is the ubiquitous Soldepeñas at a giveaway price. The wine list is short but sufficient, with a dozen familiar Rioja reds, two whites and two rosés. Again the prices are divided, half being ordinary and half more expensive, including a Faustino 1 *gran reserva*.

José said he gets a lot of regular foreign trade. We weren't at all surprised. This part of the Axarquía, near the Viñuela reservoir, is a very scenic area of rolling hills and gently winding roads less than an hour's drive from Málaga city. Lunch at the Zalia, a model venta in many ways, makes a pleasant finish to an easy day trip.

⑤⓪ VENTA EL PILAR *

Carretera Málaga-Moclinejo, Km. 10, Moclinejo.
Telephone 952 400 507.
Open year round from 8.30am to 2am.
No closing day.
No credit cards accepted.

The Málaga ring road, N-340/E-15, has certainly opened up the hinterlands of the eastern Costa del Sol. For this trip, take it to the Rincón de la Victoria exit which mentions Benagalbon, turn on to road MA-107, and follow the signs to Moclinejo. El Pilar, owned by Zaida Roman, the cook, and managed by her son, Juan Andrés, sits a few metres beyond the first "Route of the Raisin" road sign.

The venta seems small, but it is not. One enters through a courtyard dotted with tables under awnings. This area alone could accommodate 150 people without crowding. Beside it is a shaded veranda for another 50 or 60 customers and beyond that is a 10-seater bar and the entry to a very large dining-room filled with a fascinating array of artifacts. Brass utensils prevail, but there are stuffed animals, all sorts of tools for farm and kitchen and many pictures, including a small reproduction of the Nude Maja. Along one wall are stacked nine large barrels of the local wine of different types.

This is a good place to try two Andalusian specialties – *ajo blanco* (garlic soup served cold with green grapes) and *migas* (fried bits of bread, here served with *chorizo* sausage). Both can be recommended and aren't too garlicky here. I had the roast lamb, recommended as a house speciality and served in a thick, rich gravy rather than *au*

*ju*s. My companion had a nice piece of pork loin with her *migas*. We didn't have a meal of the day, but Juan Andrés reckoned it would always be cheap enough to get into our cheapest category.

I love the name of the house wine – Buqué. The wine list is uncomplicated, featuring Campo Viejo, Preferido and the Buqué. The local wine is strong and comes in a variety of sweet flavours and is not for drinking with your meal, though a glass to settle it afterwards is pleasant.

After a leisurely lunch we wandered down a part of the "Route of the Raisin" and the "Route of the Sun and the Avocado". Both are quite scenic and present many photo opps. They say that the views of Málaga bay from Moclinejo are spectacular, especially at night, but the winding road home and the good village wine made staying until dark an impractical option for this trip.

Seville Seville Cordoba,

Restaurante
Venta
Los Cazaores
52

Restaurante
Venta Antonio
51

Jerez

Cádiz

Estepona Marbella

Gibraltar

Alijar 137 A
C 440 22 JEREZ
23 DE LA FRONTERA
Silo

Restaurante
Venta Antonio
51

Ermª de
S. Cristóbal
124
14
San Martos
21 21 Doña Blanca
Managra EL PUERTO
bravia
El Ancla

Marchena
SE 218
SE 217 SE 70
SE 216
Parades
13 Montepal
52
Saladillo
Las Monjas
Restaurante/Venta
Los Cazaores
zalejo Bill
151 18 20
225
A 92

122

Córdoba

Jaén

53 Venta/Braserio
Las Palmeras

Antequera

Loja

54
Venta Riofrio

Granada

Málaga

Canadillas

Rute

E.
de Iznata

Encinas
Reales

Vadofresno

Torremolinos

44

53

Venta – Braserio
Las Palmeras

Fuengirola

Motril

La Parilla

55 Venta La Luna

Barrio de Enmedio

Villanueva de Algaidas

dilla

La Laguna

de Tapia

Venta Sta Barbara

Bobadilla

92

Huétor

Loja 1025

os Infier

Estac
de Sali
aguna

54
Venta Riofrio

Camacho

Cabras

Cerro

Torre

Vélez de Benaudalla

dilla

25

657

Escale

Sierra

Lújar

Rú

29

Venta La Luna

Motri

Jolúcar

Gual

4

oreña

Pue

Puntalon

336

Carchuna

N-340

Punta Car

Calahono

⑤① RESTAURANTE VENTA ANTONIO ***

Carretera Jerez-Sanlucar, Km. 5, Jeréz de la Frontera (Cádiz).
Telephones 956 140 535 & 141 403. Fax 956 140 535.
Open year round from1.30 to 5pm and 8pm to midnight.
No closing day.
Credit cards: all cards accepted.

This elegant eating place would be considered a first-class restaurant anywhere in the world. Make no mistake, however. Congenial owner Antonio García Archidona considers his establishment to be a venta. The best venta he can possibly make it, to be sure, but a venta all the same. In this location for 15 years, he formerly owned the now defunct Venta Los Naranjos just down the road.

The first thing you notice is the enormous parking lot, big enough for a formula one race. There is shaded parking for an awful lot of cars. You enter the large single-storied building under an arch and through a beautifully planted courtyard with a small water well in its centre. You then enter a large U-shaped bar which is apparently never entirely empty of customers.

From there you normally proceed to the "everyday" dining-room seating 125 guests. It is a quietly ornate Andalusian venue with heavily beamed ceilings mounted with soft baby spotlights, a functional central fountain, wrought iron dividers splitting the room approximately into thirds, pink striped curtains and sturdy green plants in the corners. It's rich. There are also private dining-rooms seating 30 and 60 people and a banquet facility which can accommodate 500.

Not surprisingly, there is no meal of the day here and the cheapest one we could construct from the menu was well above the minimum of what we consider the expen-

sive category for ventas. To keep things in perspective, however, a house speciality will probably cost you less than any meal at many of the well-known restaurants in the coast's seaside towns.

Going with the recommendations of our waiter Sebastian, a García employee for 25 years, we had two fish dishes you wouldn't normally see in a venta: *corvina*, which is croaker, grilled, and *urta*, which is, well, *urta*, in a casserole. Both were delicate and would be enjoyed, we believe, even by people who don't normally order fish. The menu, in Spanish and English, contains some 30 fish items as well as eight meat entrees.

The wine list features wines of the area, including all brands of *fino* and *Manzanilla* sherry, and more than 15 quality reds at the upper end of coast prices. We had the moderately priced Tierra Blanca white, from the José Paez Morilla Bodegas in Cádiz, and it accompanied our fish beautifully.

㉢ VENTA LOS CAZAORES ✱✱✱

Ctra. Antequerra-Sevilla (A-92), Km. 55.5, Marchena (Sevilla).
Telephone 954 847 698.
Open year round from 6am till midnight.
No closing day.
Closed 2 days in Aug. or Sept. for the Marchena fair.
Credit cards: Visa, 4B, Mastercard.

The name is not misspelled. The "d" was intentionally left out of Los Cazaores (The Hunters) because there was already a restaurant called Los Cazadores in Seville. The beauty of it is that omitting the "d" couldn't be more typically Andaluz since in these parts it's done all the time. I love the appropriateness of it.

My sidekick and I love the restaurant, too, since we each had one of the better venta meals we consumed while researching this book. Miguel Bremes Santos, the cordial and helpful waiter told us Los Cazaores has been open at this location for 10 years. Each of the two owners runs the business for two years and then hands over to the other.

The big, U-shaped bar is a pleasant dining area for the majority of weekday customers, seating about 60. For fair weather dining, there is a veranda fronting on a green garden, which Miguel says will accommodate as many customers as come on the busiest Sunday. We ate in the more intimate formal dining-room beside, but completely apart from, the bar. It's pleasantly decorated, the main features being a large oil painting of a greyhound chasing a rabbit, a non-functional fireplace and a Seville ceiling.

Given the name of the place, we were obviously going to have game, which not surprisingly is the speciality here. The specials on the day we were there were rabbit

with garlic and partridge in a pepper sauce, the top of the line at this venta but not that expensive compared to coast prices. I had the latter. It was fresh from the hunt, and superb. My companion had an item from the meal of the day, hare with rice – a full meal, delicious and quite inexpensive. As ventas go, Los Cazaores is not cheap. The meal of the day – not available as such in the dining-room – is just over the top of our moderate category.

The house wine, an inexpensive Valdepeñas, varies depending upon price and availability. The wine list is very short, featuring half a dozen red Riojas and a couple each whites and rosés, all at approximately coast prices. We had a Viña Eguia 1989 crianza from Domecq's Alavesa vineyards, which was fine with our meal.

Driving the some 150 not-terribly-scenic kilometres from Málaga city to Los Cazaores just to have lunch is not a great idea. It is a fine place to eat but there are dozens of others a lot closer and more fun to get to. However, if you are heading up that way on a trip, I doubt that you could find a better place for your first lunch break.

㊆ VENTA/BRASERIA LAS PALMERAS *

Ctra. Malaga-Córdoba (N-331), Km. 80, Lucena (Córdoba).
Telephone 957 251 5267.
Open year round from 9am to midnight.
No closing day.
No credit cards accepted.

You can't miss Las Palmeras because, though the front of
the place is deceptively small and somewhat unattractive,
its presence is announced by at least half a dozen signs of
various sizes and colour combinations. Be warned, however, that only one of these proclaims it to be a venta, and
that's the one facing the traffic coming from Cordoba.

You enter through a tiny bar (apparently only used at
busy times) into a bright dining-room with 25 or so tables,
mostly placed close together, but with several to one side
in front of a fireplace. The wood used for fuel was broken-
up wine barrels. The walls are colourfully decorated with
fans, tiles, plates, various tools and implements and the
windows set off with Alpujarra curtains.

Beyond the first dining area is the working bar, full of
artifacts and things for sale, such as holiday gift baskets,
hams, six-packs of Montilla-Moriles wine, key chains,
ceramic stuff, sweets related to Spanish fiestas, and pen-
nants featuring the logos of various Spanish football
clubs. Beyond this bar is a second dining area – at least
as big as the first– which is used when there's a crowd.
Outside, there are 20 or more tables for dining al fresco
amongst numerous old wine barrels.

As the name suggests, the Venta/Braseria Las
Palmeras features grilled items, of which about 20 are
listed on the menu (in Spanish only). We had the ribs of

suckling pig (tender and delicate) and grilled lamb, a combination of ribs and chops (not quite as tender, but extremely flavourful). The meat was served with chips and an unusual cabbage salad. If you prefer seafood, there are seven offerings on the bill of fare, plus the usual salads, soups and eggs.

Manuel Alba is another owner who apparently doesn't believe in wine lists, but there is a selection available. We were satisfied with the house wine, our old venta friend Soldepeñas. If you're not, you'll just have to ask Salvador Cobos, the factotum during the week, to run through the list. Be sure to ask the prices, as the Soldepeñas cost more than we usually pay. The meal of the day, however, was comfortably inside our inexpensive range.

As we walked out, full of good food, we passed the case with the *turrones, pulverones, mantecados* and a gift box of two bottles of *cava* and two fancy glasses for sale.

"You know," I said, "There's a word for a place like this."

My constant companion nodded. "Funky," she said.

"That's the word," I replied.

"But nice," she said.

"Absolutely," I agreed.

⑭ VENTA RIOFRIO ***

Autovia Málaga-Granada (A-92), Km. 197, Riofrio (Granada).
Telephones 958 321 066 & 958 322 151.
Open year round from 8am to midnight.
No closing day.
Credit cards: all cards accepted.

Although the menu is vast – with not only a meal of the
day (expensive by our calculations) but also a plate of the
day, which is cheap and will do for a light lunch by itself –
you come to this place for one thing: the trout. It is served
here seven or eight different ways, all of which will be
explained to you in English by one of the staff.

The Venta Riofrio has been in business for more than
30 years. As befits a landmark, its vast parking lot may
be accessed directly from the autovía, a rare privilege.
There are two distinct venues, side by side, inside the
same building. All customers enter by the same door, into
a rather garish, honky-tonk-type cafeteria with a long,
self-service cafeteria counter facing seven or eight picnic-
style tables which can accommodate 60 or 70.

At one end is a well-stocked souvenir counter. At the
other end is the entrance to a large and tastefully appoint-
ed eating area. Riofrio caters to coach groups that seem to
enjoy the camaraderie of cheek to cheek eating in the cafeteria. We prefer the more sedate and conventional dining-
room, which is where four of us ate – trout, of course.

The dining-room, dividable into several areas by means
of folding doors, can accommodate as many as 600 people.
On normal days, they fill the first area initially and that
is where we sat, in a neat but plain room, with salmon-

coloured drapes and table cloths and a serving table embellished with fruit plates and crockery.

We all chose the meal of the day, being there primarily for the *trucha arco iris*. We had it *con almendras* (in an almond sauce), *a la Genovesa* (in a sauce made of chopped ham with garlic and parsley), *a la Navarra* (with Serrano ham in the cavity) and *frito* (just plain fried). Arguments endured most of the way home as to which was the tastiest but, really, we couldn't fault any of the dishes.

The wine list is enormous, with something for all preferences and budgets, but the house Guerola white, from the Bodegas Miguel Martín in Valdepeñas, is remarkably inexpensive and gets the job done quite well.

If you like trout and happen to be on the Granada road, you should stop at Riofrio, the village devoted to the serving of that gastronomic treat. There are at least six restaurants here which will serve you the noble fish in a variety of surroundings and prepared in any of the known ways. The Venta Riofrio, however, is the biggest, the easiest to get to and arguably the best.

㊝ VENTA LA LUNA ***

Carretera las Ventillas, s/n, Km. 2, Motril (Granada).
Telephone 958 825 529 .
Open year round from 1.30pm till last customer leaves.
No closing day.
Credit cards: Visa, Mastercard, Eurocard.

We first heard about La Luna from a man in the Motril townhall who said it was the only venta in that area he could personally recommend. To get there, turn left off N-340 just past the Km. 334 sign. Two kilometres up that street you will see a Cepsa/Elf gas station on your left and many signposts facing you. Turn right (towards Los Tablones and elsewhere) and in two more kilometres, there's La Luna.

This venta is really three different places: a big saloon with two bars, an electronic dart board and a *tertulia* (chat) corner; a summer garden with its own bar; and an intimate dining-room. Only the last-named concerns us here. Seating only 40 patrons, this room is judiciously decorated, the most striking feature being the use of rough bricks partially covering the old walls and support columns. Unusual ceramics, original oil paintings by a friend of owner Ricardo Lopez González, and a deer's head over the large fireplace are charming additions.

The menu is quite small. In winter, only six starters and nine meat dishes are offered. There are no fish dishes. That is by no means as Spartan as it might sound. A tomato/egg/celery salad with creamy dressing was presented to us on the house. I had near-perfect garlic soup and a delightful veal steak with mushroom sauce. My companion had scalloped pork with a refreshingly mild pepper sauce.

After dinner, we were presented with two glasses of a liqueur charmingly named Grandmother's Custard, also on the house. Ricardo doesn't have a formal meal of the day, but his wife, Mercedes, who is the cook, says she can do one for 900 pesetas, but our meal cost much more..

I declined the house wine – an unspecified "this year's" Rioja – mainly because the short wine list was intriguing, with almost all new names. I tried the Bacasis from Avinya in the new Pla de Bagis region and was glad I did, even though the 1995 vintage is still much too young. Being in a seaside town, it did not surprise me that the wine at La Luna is not cheap.

La Luna is not only a great lunch stop if you are heading farther east, it is also a perfectly reasonable destination for a day trip. The spectacular sea views from the curving, elevated highway, between Nerja and Motril, make the trip worthwhile and, no matter what you may think of the local method of cultivating fruit and vegetables under plastic, the view from on high of the Plastic Coast is awesome and unforgettable.

WHAT'S AVAILABLE WHERE

So you fancy lamb chops at a venta today? Well, here's an alphabetical list that tells you where you can eat good lamb chops as well as other popular venta dishes. I have not tried all of these items in all of these places, but if you are looking for a particular type of venta food this list should help you find it.

Barbecued meat
Antigua Venta de Alfarnate, Los Arcos, Los Conejitos, El Cortijo, El Jinete, Los Morenos, Las Palmeras (Cordoba), Los Pilotos, La Rivera, Talillas, El Tintero Campero.

Bean soup
Galwey, El Pozo.

Boar in sauce
Galwey, Los Olivos.

Chicken in a pot
San Juan.

Chicken in special sauce
Los Almendros, La Porrita, Venta la Torre.

Chicken livers
Torre de Vega.

Chicken thighs
Rio Grande.

Chicken, young
San Juan

Fish/Shellfish, fresh
Antonio, Los Arcos, El Tintero Campero.

Fried fish platter
Los Almendros.

Gambas pil-pil (seasoned shrimp in hot oil)
Los Conejitos, El Cortijo.

Game in general
Los Almendros, Los Cazaores, Los Olivos.

Goat
Antigua Venta de Alfarnate, Los Arrieros, Patascortas, San Miguel, Zalia.

Goat stew
El Caserío.

Ham in sauce
Antigua Venta de Alfarnate, Los Pilotos.

Kabob
El Jinete, La Porrita, El Tintero Campero.

Kid
El Caserio, Cozar, Galwey, Vazquez.

Lamb chops
Los Arrieros, Atanores, Los Cabales, Cozar, Las Palmeras (Cordoba), Pula, El Tintero Campero.

Lamb, roasted
Los Cabales, El Caserio, Manolo, El Pilar, Los Pinso del Coto, El Punto, Los Reales, El Tintero Campero, Venta la Torre, Trillo.

Lamb stew
Los Arrieros, Los Olivos, Severino, Venta la Torre.

Lasagne (homemade)
San Miguel.

Migas
Antigua Venta de Alfarnate, Los Arrieros, Atanores, Cotrina (Sun. & fiestas), Fuente de la Higuera (Sun. & fiestas), Galwey, Patascortas (Sun.), El Pilar, La Rivera, Romeral del Rocio, Severino.

Oxtail stew
Los Arrieros, Las Palmeras (Córdoba), Patascortas, El Pozo, Romeral del Rocio, Venta la Torre.

Paella
Barranco, Los Cazaores (six people minimum, by order), Los Condes, Cotrina, Manolo, Las Palmeras (Coin), Patascortas (Sunday or by order), Platero, Rio Grande (two people minimum), Romeral del Rocio, Severino (two people minimum), Sierra Mijas.

Partridge
Los Almendros, Los Arrieros, Los Cazaores, El Cortijo, La Yedra.

Peppers, stuffed
El Mirador (Antequera), Sierra Mijas.

Pig's knuckle
Antigua Venta de Alfarnate, El Mirador (Antequera), Los Pinos del Coto.

Pork chops, baby
Manolo, Las Palmeras (Córdoba), El Punto, Zalia.

Pork ribs
El Mirador (Ronda), Los Morenos, Los Olivos, El Pozo.

Pork, stuffed
El Mirador (Ronda), Rio Grande.

Porra/salmorejo (thick gazpacho)
Los Arrieros, El Cordobés, El Mirador (Antequera), Talilla.

Quail
Los Arrieros, Las Palmeras (Córdoba), El Punto, Rio Grande, San Miguel.

Rabbit in a pot
San Juan.

Rabbit (whole)
Barranco.

Salmon (fresh)
Los Arcos

Snails
Platero, La Porrita, Rio Grande, Severino, Torre la Vega.

Trout
Rio Frio, La Vega, La Yedra.

Tuna (fresh)
Los Arcos, Los Cabales.

Veal cutlet
El Caserio, El Limonar, Los Pilotos.

Venison
Los Almendros, Cozar, La Vega.

All of the above are subject to availability and, of course, changes in menus.

I have not listed the following great favorites because they are always on hand in most ventas:

Callos (chickpea stew with pork bits).
Chicken or rabbit with garlic (pollo o conejo con ajo).
Magro (pork cubes over chips/fries).
Meatballs (albóndigas).
Pork chop (chuleta de cerdo).
Pork stew (estofado).
Pork tenderloin (lomo or solomillo).
Soup stew of the day or the area (ask what's in it).
Veal steak (filete de ternera).

WHAT A DISH!

Here is an alphabetical list of my favourite dishes together with the ventas that do them especially well.

Berenjena con Miel de Caña
(eggplant slices deepfried & flavoured with honey) at Antigua Venta de Alfarnate, page 112.

Conejo al Ajillo
(garlic rabbit) at Venta Los Conejitos, page 48.

Cordero Asado
(roast lamb) at Venta Los Reales, page 22.

Cordero a la Pastoril
(lamb shepherd's style) at Venta Los Olivos, page 104.

Costillas
(pork ribs) at Venta El Pozo, page 66.

Costillitas de Chivo al Ajillo
(tiny kid ribs with garlic) at Venta Cozar, page 18.

Gambas Pil-Pil
(shrimp in sizzling spicy oil) at Los Conejitos, page 48.

Jabalí en Salsa de Almendras
(wild boar in almond sauce) at Venta Galwey, page 106.

Jamon Asado al Vino de Los Montes
(ham done in wine of the mountains) at Antigua Venta de Alfarnate, page 112.

Liebre con Arroz
(hare with rice) at Venta Los Cazaores, page 126.

Lomo al Ajillo
(pork tenderloin in garlic) at Venta Los Pilotos, page 54.

Lomo de Cerdo en Taco

(pork tenderloin) at Venta La Yedra, page 60.

Magro de Tomate
(pork cubes in tomato sauce) at Venta Torre Vega, page 76.

Manito de Cerdo
(pig's knuckle) at Venta El Mirador (Antequera), page 56.

Migas
(fried breadcrumbs) at Venta Los Atanores, page 52.

Patatas Fritas
(french fried potatoes/chips) at Venta La Porrita, page 74.

Peras en Vino Tinto
(pears in red wine) at Venta Cozar, page 18.

Perdiz en Salsa
(partridge in sauce) at Venta Los Cazaores, page 126.

Pimientos Rellenos Navarra
(stuffed peppers) at Venta Sierra Mijas, page 96.

Pollo Ajillo
(chicken in garlic) at Venta La Porrita, page 74.

Porra la Antequerana
(thick gazpacho) at Venta El Cordobés, page 42.

Rabo de Toro
(oxtail) at Venta El Pozo, page 66.

Smoked Delights
(hors d'oeuvre) at Venta Los Pinos del Coto, page 82.

Trucha
(trout,any of several ways) at Venta Riofrio, page 130.

WHAT THE VENTA NAMES MEAN

1 Venta Cozar – family name.

2 Venta Manolo – owner's nickname.

3 Venta Los Reales – the camp grounds.

4 Venta San Juan – saint's name.

5 Venta La Vega – area name.

6 Venta El Mirador (Ronda) – the lookout point.

7 Venta Los Almendros – the almond trees.

8 Venta El Caserio – the country home.

9 Venta Barranco – family name.

10 Venta Pula – area name.

11 Venta Rio Grande – name of adjacent river.

12 Venta Cordobés – name of bullfighter Manuel Benitez.

13 Venta El Punto – the peak, top.

14 Venta Trillo – the thresher.

15 Venta Los Conjitos – the little rabbits (family nickname).

16 Venta Fuente de la Higuera – fountain of the fig tree.

17 Venta Los atanores – arab name for water pipes.

18 Venta Los Pilotos – the pilots.

19 Venta El Mirador (Antequera) – lookout point.

20 Venta La Rivera – family name.

21 Venta La Yedra – the ivy.

22 Ventorillo Patascortas – short feet (family nickname).

23 Venta Cotrina – area name.

24 Venta El Pozo – the well.

25 Venta El Limonar – the lemon grove.

26 Venta Romeral del Rocio – dewy rosemary field.

27 Venta El Tintero Campero – the country inkwell.

28 Venta La Porrita – the little hammer.

29 Venta Torre de Vega – family name.

30 Venta Severino – family nickname.

31 Venta Vazquez – family name.

32 Venta Los Pinos del Coto – area name.

33 Venta Los Cabales – the select ones.

34 Venta Los Arocs – the arches.

35 Venta Platero – area name.

36 Venta Las Palmeras (Coín) – the palm trees.

37 Venta Los Morenos – family name.

38 Venta Los Condes – area name.

39 Venta Sierra Mijas – area name.

40 Venta La Torre – the tower.

41 Venta El Jinete – the horseman.

42 Venta Los Olivos – the olive trees.

43 Venta Galwey – named after an English traveller.

44 Venta Los Arrieros – the firewood sellers.

45 Venta San Miguel – saint's name.

46 Antigua Venta de Alfarnate – area name.

47 Venta Talillas – family nickname.

48 Venta El Cortijo – the farmhouse.

49 Venta Zalia – area name.

50 Venta El Piilar – area name.

51 Restaurante Venta Antonio – given name of owner.

52 Venta Los Cazaores – the hunters.

53 Venta Braserio Las Palmeras – the palm trees.

54 Venta Riofrio – area name.

55 Venta La Luna – the moon.

GLOSSARY

A la brasa (ah lah BRAH-sah) – cooked over coals
aceitunas (ah-say-TOO-nahs) – olives
adobado (ah-doe-BAH-doe) – pickled
agua con gas (ah-gwah cawn gahs) – fizzy water
agua sin gas (ah-gwah seen gahs) – still water
alioli (a-lee-oh-lee) – garlic mayonnaise
ajetes (ah-HAY-tay) – garlic sprouts
ajo (AH-hoe) – garlic
ajo blanco (AH-hoe blonk-oh) – garlic soup
albaricoque (ahl-bah-ree-KO-kay) – apricot
albóndigas (ahl-BON-dee-gahs) – meatballs
alitas de pollo (ah-LEE-tahs day poy-yo) – chicken wings
almejas (ahl-MAY-hahs) – small clams
almendra (ahl-MEN-drah) – almond
almond – almendra (ahl-MEN-drah)
almuerzo (ahl-mwer-so) – lunch
anchovies, fried – boquerones fritos (bo-kay-RO-
        nays free-toes)
anchovies, marinated – boquerones en vinagre (bo-kay-
        RO-nays en vee-nah-gray)
apple – manzana (mahn-zah-nah)
apricot – albaricoque (ahl-bah-ree-KO-kay)
arroz (ah-rohth) – rice; also paella
arroz con leche (ah-rohth cawn lay-chay) – rice pudding
asado (ah-sah-doe) – roasted
aseo (ah-SAY-oh) – toilet, bathroom
atún (ah-TOON) – tuna
aubergine — berenjena (bair-en-HAY-nah)
aves (AH-vays) – birds, fowl
azucar (ah-ZU-kar) – sugar

142

Barbacoa (bar-bah-KO-ah) – barbecue

barbecue – barbacoa (bar-bah-KO-ah)

barbecued – a la parilla (ah lah pah-REE-yah)

bass, sea – lubina (loo-BEEN-ah)

bean , broad— haba (AH- bah)

bean, green – judía verde (who-DEE-a vair-day)

beef steak – bistek (bee-stake), entrecote (ahn-tray-
        COAT), filete de buey (fee-LAY-tay day bway)

beer – cerveza (sair-VAY-sah)

beer on tap – cerveza de barril (day ba-reel) or caña (can-ya)

berenjena (bair-en-HAY-nah) aubergine – eggplant

berza (BAIR-sah) – cabbage

bién dorados (bee-en doe-RAH-dose) – well done (as in chips)

bién hecho (bee-en EH-cho) – well done (as in meats)

birds – aves (AH-vays)

bistek (bee-stake) – beef steak

blackberry – mora (mor-ah)

blanco (blonk-oh) - white; white wine

boar (wild) – jabalí (hah-bah-LEE)

bocadillo (bo-kah-DEE-yo) – sandwich

boquerones al vinagre (bo-kay-RO-nays ahl vee-nah-
        gray) – marinated anchovies

boquerones fritos (bo-kay-RO-nays free-toes) – fried anchovies

bourbon whiskey – whisky americano (wiss-kee ah-mair-
        ee-kah-no)

brandy, Spanish – coñac (cawn-yak)

braseria - (brah-say-REE-ah) – restaurant specializing in
        meats cooked over coals

bread— pan (pahn)

breaded veal cutlet with ham – escalope san jacobo (es-
        kah-LO-pay sahn hah-KO-bo)

breaded veal cutlet with ham and cheese – escalope cordon
        bleu (es-kah-LO-pay kor-dawn blew)

breakfast – desayuno (day-sah-YU-no)

breast (as in chicken) – pechuga (pay-CHU-gah)
broth – consomé (kon-soh-MAY)

Cabbage – berza (BAIR-sah); coles (ko-les)
cabrito (kah-BREE-toe) – kid
café con leche (kah-fay cawn lay-chay)— coffee with milk
café solo (kah-fay so-lo) – coffee, black
cajero (ka-hair-ro) – cashier
caldereta (kahl-day-RAY-tah) – stew
calamares (kahl-ah-MAH-rays) – squid
caliente (kal-ee-EN-tay) – hot
callos (ky-yos) – tripe (usually more chickpeas & pork
          bits than tripe)
caña (kahn-yah) – small glass of draft beer
cangrejo (kan-GRAY-ho) – crab
caracoles (kah-rah-KO-les) — snails
carne (kar-nay) – meat
carrots – zanahorias (zan-ah-OR-ee-ahs)
carta (kar-tah) – printed food menu
carta de vinos (kar-tah day vee-nos) – wine list
casero (kah-sair-oh) – home-made
cashier – cajero (ka-hair-ro)
casserole – cazuela (kah-zwe-lah)
cava (kah-vah) – Spanish sparkling wine
caza (kah-zah) – wild game
cazuela (kah-zwe-lah) – casserole
cebolla (say-BOY-yah) – onion
cena (say-nah) – dinner; supper
cerdo (sair-doe) – pork
cerveza (sair-VAY-sah) – beer
cerveza de barril (sair-Vay-sah day ba-reel) – beer on tap
champaña (shahm-PAHN-yah) – French champagne
champagne (French) – champana (sham-PAHN-yah)
champagne (Spanish) – cava (kah-vah)
champñones (sham-pin-YO-nays) – mushrooms

cheese – queso (kay-so)
chickpeas – garbanzos (gar-BAHN-zoes)
chicken – pollo (poy-yo)
chicken thighs – muslos de pollo (mooz-los day poy-yo)
chicken wings – alas de pollo (a-LAHS day poy-yo)
chili pepper – pimiento picante (pee-mee-EN-toe
    pee-KAHN-tay)
chips (French fries) – patatas fritas (pah-TAH-
    tahs free-tahs)
chivo (chee-vo) – goat
chocolate – chocolate (chah-ko-LAH-tay)
chop – chuleta (chu-LAY-tah)
chorizo (cho-REE-so) – spicy Spanish sausage
chuleta (chu-LAY-tah) – chop
chuleton (chu-lay-TONE) – king-sized chop
churrasco (chu-RAH-sko) – barbecued meat
clams, small – almejas (ahl-MAY-hahs)
clara (klah-rah) – shandy
cochinillo (ko-chee-NEE-yo) – suckling pig
cocido (ko-SEE-doe) – stew
codillo (ko-dee-yo) – pig's knuckle
codorniz (ko-dor-neece) – quail
coffee, black - café solo (kah-fay so-lo)
coffee with milk — café con leche (kah-fay cawn
    lay-chay)
cognac, French – coñac francés (cawn-yak frahn-ses)
cold — frio (free-oh)
coles (ko-les) – cabbage
comida (ko-MEE-dah) – meal; food
coñac (cawn-yak) – brandy (Spanish}
coñac francés (cawn-yak frahn-ses) – French cognac
conejo (ko-NAY-ho) – rabbit
consomé (kon-soh-MAY) – broth; consommé
consommé – comsomé (kon-soh-MAY)
cordero (kor-DAIR-oh) – lamb
costillas (kos-TEE-yahs) – spareribs

crab – cangrejo (kan-gray-ho)
custard, caramel — flan (flahn)
custard, vanilla — natillas (nah-TEE-yahs)
cuttlefish – jíbia (HIB-ee-yah)

De la casa (day lah KAH-sah) – of the house (as in
    salad, wine, etc.)
deep-fried – frito en aceite abundante (free-toe en ah-
    SAY-tay ah-bun-dahn-tay)
desayuno (day-sah-YU-no) – breakfast
dessert – postre (post-ray)
dinner – cena (say-nah)

Egg – huevo (way-vo)
eggplant – berenjena (bair-en-HAY-nah)
ensalada (en-sah-LAH-dah) – salad
entrecote (ahn-tray-COAT) – beef steak
entremeses (ahn-tray-may-ses) – first course
escabechado (es-cah-bay-CHAH-doe) – pickled, marinated
escalope cordon bleu (es-kah-LO-pay kor-dawn blew) —
    breaded veal cutlet with ham and cheese (some-
    times pork)
escalope san jacobo (es-kah-LO-pay sahn hah-KO-bo) –
    breaded veal cutlet with ham
especialidad de la casa (es-pesh-ee-ahl-ee-dahd day lah
    KAH-sah) – house specialty
estofado (es-toe-fah-doe) – stew

Filete de buey (fee-LAY-tay day bway) – beef steak
filete de cerdo (fee-LAY-tay day sair-doe) – pork steak
filete de ternera (fee-LAY-tay day tair-nay-rah) – veal
    (young beef) steak
fino (fee-no) — sherry, dry

first course (starter) – primer plato (pree-mair plah-toe)
fish - pescado (pes-SKAH-doe)
fish, fried, variety – fritura malagueña (free-TU-rah
     mah-lah-GAIN-yah)
flan (flahn) – egg caramel
food – comida (ko-MEE-dah)
fowl – aves (AH-vays)
frambuesa (fram-BWAY-sah) – raspberry
fresa (FRAY-sah) – strawberry
fried – frito (free-toe)
fried in batter – rebozado (ray-bo-ZAH-doe)
frío (free-oh) – cold
frito (free-toe) – fried
fritura malagueña (free-TU-rah mahl-ah-GAIN-ya) –
     fried fish platter
fruit – fruta (fru-tah)
fruta (fru-tah) – fruit
frutas del mar (fru-tahs del mar) – seafood

Gambas (gahm-bahs) – shrimps
gambas pil-pil (gahm-bahs pill-pill) – shrimps in hot spicy oil
game, wild – caza (kah-zah)
garbanzos (gar-BAHN-zoes) – chick peas
garlic – ajo (AH-ho)
garlic mayonnaise – alioli (a-lee-oh-lee)
garlic soup, cold – ajo blanco (AH-ho blonk-oh)
garlic sprouts – ajetes (ah-HAY-tays)
gazpacho (gahz-pah-cho) – cold tomato soup with season-
     ing; also see porra antequerana and salmorejo
goat – chivo (chee-vo)
grape – uva (OO-vah)
grifo, al (GREE-foe, ahl) – on tap (as in beer)
grilled – a la plancha (ah-lah-PLAHN-cha)
guiso (ghee-so(- stew

Hake – merluza (mair-lu-za)
ham – jamón (hah-MON)
ham, cured – jamón serrano (hah-MON sair-RAH-no)
ham and beans – fabada (far-bar-dar)
ham, fresh with garlic – lomo al ajillo (lo-mo ahl ah-HEE-yo)
ham with melon – jamón con melón (hah-MON con mel-LON)
helado (eh-LAH-doe) – ice cream
hielo (ee-el-oh) – ice
home-fried potatoes – patatas a lo pobre (pah-TAH-tahs ah
        lo PO-bray)
home-made – casero (kah-sair-oh)
hors d'oeuvre – tapa (tah-pah)
hot (as in seasoning) – picante (pee-KAHN-tay)
hot (as in temperature) – caliente (kal-ee-EN-tay)
house (as in salad, wine, etc.) – de la casa (day
        lah KAH-sah)
house specialty – especialidad de la casa (es-pesh-ee-ahl-
        ee-dahd day lah KAH-sah)
huevo (way-voe) – egg
huevo a la flamenca (way-vo a la fla-men-ka – fried egg with
        chorizo and peas
huevos rellenos(way-voes-ray-yay-noes — stuffed eggs

Ice — hielo (ee-el-oh)
ice cream – helado (eh-LAH-doe)

Jabalí (hah-bah-LEE) – boar (wild)
jabón (hah-BON) – soap
jamón (hah-MON) – ham
jamón con melón (hah-MON con mel-LON) – ham with melon
jamón serrano (hah-MON sair-RAH-no) – cured ham
jíbia (HIB-ee-yah) – cuttlefish

Kid – cabrito (kah-BREE-toe)

Lamb – cordero (kor-DAIR-oh)
langostinos (lang-go-STEE-nos) – prawns
lavabo (lah-vah-bow) – wash basin
leche (lay-chay) – milk
lechón (lay-CHON) – suckling pig
legumbres (lay-GOOM-brays) – vegetables
lenguado (len-gwa-doe) – sole
lentejas (len-TAY-hahs) – lentils
lentils – lentejas (len-TAY-hahs)
licor dulce (lee-cor dool-say) – liqueur
liqueur – licor dulce (lee-cor dool-say)
lomo al ajillo (lo-mo ahl ah-HEE-yo) – fresh ham
        with garlic
lomo de cerdo (lo-mo day sair-doe) – pork loin
lunch – almuerzo (ahl-mwer-so)

Magro con tomate (mah-gro cawn toe-MAH-tay) –
        diced pork in tomato sauce
main course – plato fuerte (plah-toe fwer-tay); plato
        segundo (plah-toe say-goon-doe(
manteca (mahn-tay-kah) – lard
mantequilla (mahn-tay-KEE-yah) – butter
manzana (mahn-zah-nah) – apple
marinated – adobado (ah-doe-BAH-doe)
mariscos (mah-RISK-ohs) – shellfish
mayonnaise – mayonesa (my-oh-NAY-sah)
mayonesa (my-oh-NAY-sah) – mayonnaise
mayonnaise with garlic – alioli (a-lee-oh-lee)
meal – comida (ko-MEE-dah)
meal of the day – menú del día (may-NOO del DEE-yah)
meat – carne (kar-nay)

149

meatballs – albóndigas (ahl-BON-dee-gahs)
mechada (may-cha-dah) – larded or stuffed (of meat)
melocotón (may-lo-ko-TONE) – peach
menú – carta de platos (kar-tah day plah-toes)
menú del día (may-NOO del DEE-yah) – meal of the day
merluza (mair-lu-za) – hake
mero (may-roe) – sea bass
mesa (may-sah) – table
migas (mee-gahs) – fried bits of seasoned bread
milk – leche (lay-chay)
Montilla-Moriles (mawn-tee-yah mo-ree-lays) — wine
        from Córdoba province similar to dry sherry
mora (mor-ah) – blackberry
muslos (mooz-los) – thighs (usually chicken)
muslos de cangrejo (mooz-los day kan-GRAY-ho) – bread-
        ed, deep-fried seafood in shape of chicken thigh
mushrooms– champiñones (sham-pin-YO-nays)
mushrooms, wild – setas (say-tahs)

Natillas (nah-TEE-yahs) – vanilla custard
noodle soup with ham – sopa de picadillo (so-pah day
        pee-kah-DEE-yo)
nueces (new-ay-sez) – nuts
nuts – nueces (new-ay-sez)

Octopus - pulpo (pull-po)
olives – aceitunas ah-say TOO-nahs)
omellete – tortilla (tor-TEE-yah)
omelette, Spanish style - tortilla española (tor-TEE-yah
        es-pahn-YO-la)
onion – cebolla (say-BOY-yah)
oxtail – rabo de toro (rah-bo day tor-oh)

Paella (py-EH-yah) – rice with meat/seafood

pan (pahn) – bread

parilla, a la (pah-REE-yah, ah lah) – barbecued

parillada de carne (pah-REE-yah-dah day kar-nay) –
    mixed grill

partridge – perdíz (pair-DEECE)

patatas (pah-TAH-tahs) – potatoes

patatas a lo pobre (pah-TAH-tahs ah lo PO-bray) – home-
    fried potatoes

patatas fritas (pah-TAH-tahs free-tahs) – chips, French fries

pavo (pah-vo) – turkey

peach – melocotón (may-lo-ko-TON)

pechuga (pay-CHU-gah) – breast (as in chicken)

pepper (condiment) – pimienta (pim-ee-en-tah)

peppers, fried – pimientos fritos (pim-ee-en-toes fri-toes)

peppers (hot) – pimientos picantes (pim-ee-en-toes pee-
    KAHN-tays)

peppers (sweet) – pimientos dulces (pim-ee-en-toes dool-says)

perdíz (pair-DEECE) – partridge

pescado (pay-SKAH-doe) – fish

pez espada (pez es-pah-dah) – swordfish

picante (pee-KAHN-tay) – hot, highly seasoned

picantón (pee-kan-TON) – young chicken

pichón (pee-CHON) – type of pigeon

pickled (of fish, fowl) – escabechado (es-kah-bay-CHA-doe)

pickled (of meat) – adobado (ah-doe-BAH-doe)

pigeon – pichón (pee-CHON)

pig's knuckle – codillo (ko-dee-yo)

pimienta (pim-ee-en-tah) – pepper (condiment)

pimientos fritos (pim-ee-en-toes fri-toes) – fried peppers

pimientos picantes (pim-ee-en-toes pee-KAHN-tays) –
    hot peppers

pimientos rellenos (pim-ee-en-toes ray-yay-nos) –stuffed peppers

pinchitos (pin-CHEE-toes) – pork kebabs

pineapple – piña (peen-yah)

piña (peen-yah) – pineapple
pipirrana (pip-peer-RAH-nah) – vegetable salad
pisto (pee-sto) – stewed vegetables
plancha, a la (plahn-cha, ah lah) – grilled
plato fuerte (plah-toe fwer-tay) – main course
plato segundo (plah-toe say-goon-doe) – main course
pollo (poy-yo) – chicken
pork - cerdo (sair-doe)
pork cubes in tomato sauce – magro con tomate (mah-gro
    cawn toe-MAH-tay)
pork kebabs – pinchitos (pin-CHEE-toes)
pork loin – lomo de cerdo (lo-mo day sair-doe)
porra (por-rah) – thick gazpacho (also see salmorejo)
porra antequerana (por-rah ahn-tay-kay-RAH-nah) –
    porra Antequera style
postre (post-ray) – dessert
potaje (po-TAH-hay) – soup/stew
potatoes – patatas (pah-TAH-tahs)
prawns – langostinos (lang-oh-STEE-nos)
primer plato (pree-mair plah-toe) – first course, starter
pulpo)pull-po) – octopus

Quail – codorniz (ko-dor-neece)
queso (kay-so) – cheese

Rabbit – conejo (ko-NAY-ho)
rabo de toro (rah-bo day tor-oh) – oxtail
raspberry – frambuesa (fram-BWAY-sah)
rebosado (ray-bo-sah-doe) – batter-dipped & fried
red (as in wine) – tinto (teen-toe)
rice – arroz (ah-rohth)
rice pudding) arroz con leche (ah-rohth cawn lay-chay)
roasted – asado (ah-SAH-doe)
rosado (ro-sah-doe) – fish often served as sea bass; rosé wine

Sacarina (sack-ah-ree-nah) – saccharine
saccharine – sacarina (sack-ah-ree-nah)
sal (sal) – salt
salad – ensalada (en-sah-lah-dah)
salchicha (sal-CHEE-cha) – sausage
salmon – salmón (sal-MON)
salmón (sal-MON) – salmon
salmorejo (sal-mor-RAY-ho) – thick gazpacho
salpicón de bocas del mar (sal-pee-CON day bo-kahs del
       mar) – seafood salad
salsa (sahl-sah) – sauce; gravy
salt – sal (sal)
sandía (san-DEE-yah) – watermelon
sandwich – bocadillo (bo-kah-DEE-yo)
sardinas (sar-deen-ahs) – sardines
sangría (san-GREE-ah) – red wine punch
sauce – salsa (sahl-sah)
sausage – salchicha (sal-CHEE-cha)
sausage, spicy – chorizo (cho-REE-so)
scotch whiskey – whisky escocés (wiss-kee es-ko-sace)
seafood – frutas del mar (fru-tahs del mar)
servicio, el (sair-VEE-see-oh, el) – toilet
servicios, los (sair-VEE-see-ohs, los) – toilets
shandy – clara (clah-rah)
shellfish – mariscos (mah-RISK-ohs)
sherry, dry – fino (fee-no)
shrimps – gambas (gahm-bahs)
snails – caracoles (kah-rah-KO-les)
soap – jabón (hah-BON)
sole – lenguado (len-gwa-doe)
solomillo (so-lo-MEE-yo) – tenderloin (usually pork)
sopa (so-pah) – soup
sopa de picadillo (so-pah day pee-kah-DEE-yo) – noodle
       soup with ham

sopa mondeña (so-pah mawn-dayn-yah) – vegetable
        soup/stew on bread base

sopa perota (so-pah pay-ro-tah) – similar to sopa mondeña

soup – sopa (so-pah)

soup/stew – potaje (po-TAH-hay)

spareribs – costillas (ko-STEE-yahs)

squid – calamares (kah-lah-MAH-rays)

steak (beef, pork or veal) – filete (fee-LAY-tay)

stew – caldereta (kahl-day-ret-ah); cocido (ko-SEE-doe);
        estofado (es-toe-FAH-doe); guiso (ghee-so)

strawberry – fresa (fray-sah)

stuffed (or larded) — mechada (may-CHA-dah)

suckling pig – cochinillo (ko-chee-NEE-yo); lechón (lay-
        CHON)

sugar – azucar (ah-ZU-kar)(

supper – cena (say-nah)

swordfish – pez espada (pez es-pah-dah)

Table – mesa (may-sah)

tapa (tah-pah) – hors d'oeuvre

tenderloin (usually pork) – solomillo (so-lo-MEE-yo)

tinta (TEEN-tah) – liquid from squid

tinto (TEEN-toe) – red wine

tinto de verano (teen-toe day vay-rah-no) – summer wine
        (mixture of wine & soda); wine cooler

tocino del cielo (tor-THEE-no day thee-el-o) – custard squares

toilet (bathroom) – servicio (sair-VEE-see-oh); aseo (ass-say-oh)

tomato – tomate (toe-MAH-tay)

tomate (toe-MAH-tay) – tomato

tortilla (tor-TEE-yah) – omelette

tortilla española (tor-TEE-yah es-pan- YO-la) – thick
        omelette made with eggs and potatoes

tripe – callos (ky-yos)

trout – trucha (tru-cha)

trucha (tru-cha) – trout
tuna fish – atún (ah-TOON)
turkey – pavo (pah-vo)

U va (OO-vah) – grape

V ainilla (vy-NEE-yah) – vanilla
vanilla) vainilla (vy-NEE-yah)
veal cutlet, breaded with ham – escalope san jacobo (es-
    kah-LO-pay sahn hah-KO-bo)
vegetables– legumbres (lay-GOOM-brays); verdura
    (vair-DOO-rah)
venado (vay-nah-doe) – venison
venison – carne de venado (kar-nay day vay-nah-doe)
verdura (vair-DOO-rah) – vegetables

W aiter – señor (sain-yor(for a man; señorita (sain-
    yor-ee-tah) for a woman
washbasin – lavabo (lah-vah-bow)
water, fizzy – agua con gas (ah-gwah cawn gahs)
water, still – agua sin gas (ah-gwah seen gahs)
watermelon – sandía (sahn-DEE-yah)
well done (as in chips/french fries) – bién dorados (bee-en
    doe-RAH-dose)
well done (as in meats) – bien hecho (bee-en EH-cho)
whiskey, bourbon – whisky americano (wiss-kee ah-mair-
    ee-kah-no)
whiskey, scotch – whisky escocés (wiss-kee es-ko-sace)
white (as in wine) – blanco (blonk-oh)
wine list – carta de vinos (kar-tah day vee-nos)

Z anahorias (zan-ah-OR-ee-ahs(- carrots

MORE BOOKS FROM SANTANA

You and the Law in Spain Thousands of readers have relied on this best selling book to guide them through the Spanish legal jungle. Now, there is a new, completely revised edition with even more information on taxes, work permits, cars, banking, property and lots more. It's a book no foreigner in Spain can afford to be without. *By David Searl. 224 pages.*

Cooking in Spain The definitive guide to cooking in Spain, with more than 400 great recipes. Complete information on regional specialities and culinary history, how to buy the best at the market, English-Spanish glossary and handy conversion guide. *By Janet Mendel. 376 Pages. Illustrated.*

The Best of Spanish Cooking The top food writer in Spain today invites you to a memorable feast featuring her all-time favourite Spanish recipes. More than 170 tantalizing dishes are presented, allowing you to recreate the flavour of Spain in your own home. *By Janet Mendel. 172 pages.*

Tapas and More Great Dishes from Spain This striking cookbook is a celebration of the sunny flavours of Spain - olive oil, garlic, fresh fruits and vegetables, meat and seafood -in an attractive presentation of 70 classic recipes and stunning colour photographs. *By Janet Mendel, Photographs by John James Wood. 88 pages*

Expand Your Spanish Tackle the dreaded Spanish subjunctive and chuckle at the same time? You can with this book. The author keeps you smiling as she leads you through the minefield of Spanish grammar. Not a language book in the conventional sense, but it will help you over the obstacles that put many people off learning the language. *By Linda Hall de Gonzalez. 240 pages. Illustrated.*

Excursions in Eastern Spain This guide takes you on thirty easy to follow excursions by car all over the Costa Blanca, Valencia and beyond and tells you what's worth seeing, where to stay, where to eat, how to get there and lots more. *By Nick Inman and Clara Villanueva. 272 pages.*

Excursions in Southern Spain Forty great trips through Andalusia from the twice-winner of Spain's top travel award. This handy guide will take you to the most famous sights and the least-known corners of Andalusia, Spain's most fascinating region. *By David Baird. 347 pages.*

Inside Andalusia Author David Baird invites you to explore an Andalusia you never dreamt of, to meet its people, to discover dramatic scenery and fascinating fiestas. Illustrated with brilliant colour photographs. Winner of the National Award for Travel Writing. *By David Baird. 224 pages. Illustrated.*

The Story of Spain The bold and dramatic history of Spain from the caves of Altamira to our present day. A story of kings and poets, saints and conquistadores, emperors and revolutionaries. The author has drawn on years of rigorous research to re-create the drama, excitement and pathos of crucial events in the history of the western world. *By Mark Williams. 272 pages. Illustrated.*

Andalusian Landscapes This outstanding book of colour photographs is a celebration of the astonishing collage of colours and textures in the Andalusian landscape. It captures the charm of remote villages and lonely farmhouses, fields ablaze with sunflowers and meadows full of poppies, the play of light on olive groves and the sun on the high sierras. *By Tim Gartside. 78 pages.*

Birds of Iberia Detailed descriptions of more than 150 bird species and the main habitats, migration patterns and ornithological sites. Lavishly illustrated with fine line drawings and full-colour photographs. *By Clive Finlayson and David Tomlinson. 224 pages. Large format hardback. Illustrated.*

Gardening in Spain Your most valuable tool for successful gardening in Spain. How to plan your garden, what to plant, when and how plant it, how to make the most of flowers, trees, shrubs, herbs. *By Marcelle Pitt. 216 pages. Illustrated.*

A Selection of Wildflowers of Southern Spain Southern Spain is host to a rich variety of wildflowers in widely diverse habitats, some species growing nowhere else. This book describes more than 200 common plants of the region, each illustrated in full colour with simple text for easy identification and enjoyment. *By Betty Molesworth Allen. 260 pages. Illustrated*

Shopping for Food and Wine in Spain Spain, though now an integral part of the European market, is still, happily, a little exotic. The foods and wines you find in Spanish markets are not always what you see back home. This complete guide tells you how to shop in Spain with confidence – saving you money, time and frustration. *176 pages.*

**Santana books are on sale
at bookstores in Spain
or by mail from:
Ediciones Santana S.L.,
Apartado 422
29640 Fuengirola,
(Málaga), Spain
Fax: 952 485 367
e-mail: santana@vnet.es**